STRIP BARE

SUN CITY #3

JADE CHURCH

Strip bare By Jade Church First Published in Great Britain By Jade Church in 2023

Ebook ISBN: 978-1-916522-06-0

Paperback ISBN: 978-1-916522-07-7

Se paperback ISBN: 978-1-916522-26-8

Hardback ISBN: 978-1-916522-08-4

Conditions of Sale

CONTENT WARNING

Strip Bare contains themes and content that some readers may find triggering, this includes: *references to anxiety, neurodiversity, alcohol and drug use, on-page sex, and swearing.*

ALSO BY JADE CHURCH

Standalones:

Temper the Flame

This Never Happened

Three Kisses More

Sun City (Interconnected standalones):

Get Even

Fall Hard

Strip Bare

Living in Cincy (Interconnected standalones):

In Too Deep

Tempt My Heart

Kingdom of Stars:

The Lingering Dark (Kingdom of Stars #1)

Ashvale:

Ashvale: The Vampire's Thrall

Coming Soon:

One Last Touch

The Clarity of Light (Kingdom of Stars #2)

Ashvale: The Vampire's Kiss

Keep in touch!

Don't want to miss new release details, behind the scenes sneak peeks, cover reveals, sales, and more? Then sign up to my newsletter to get swoony romance updates straight to your inbox!

https://linktr.ee/authorjadechurch

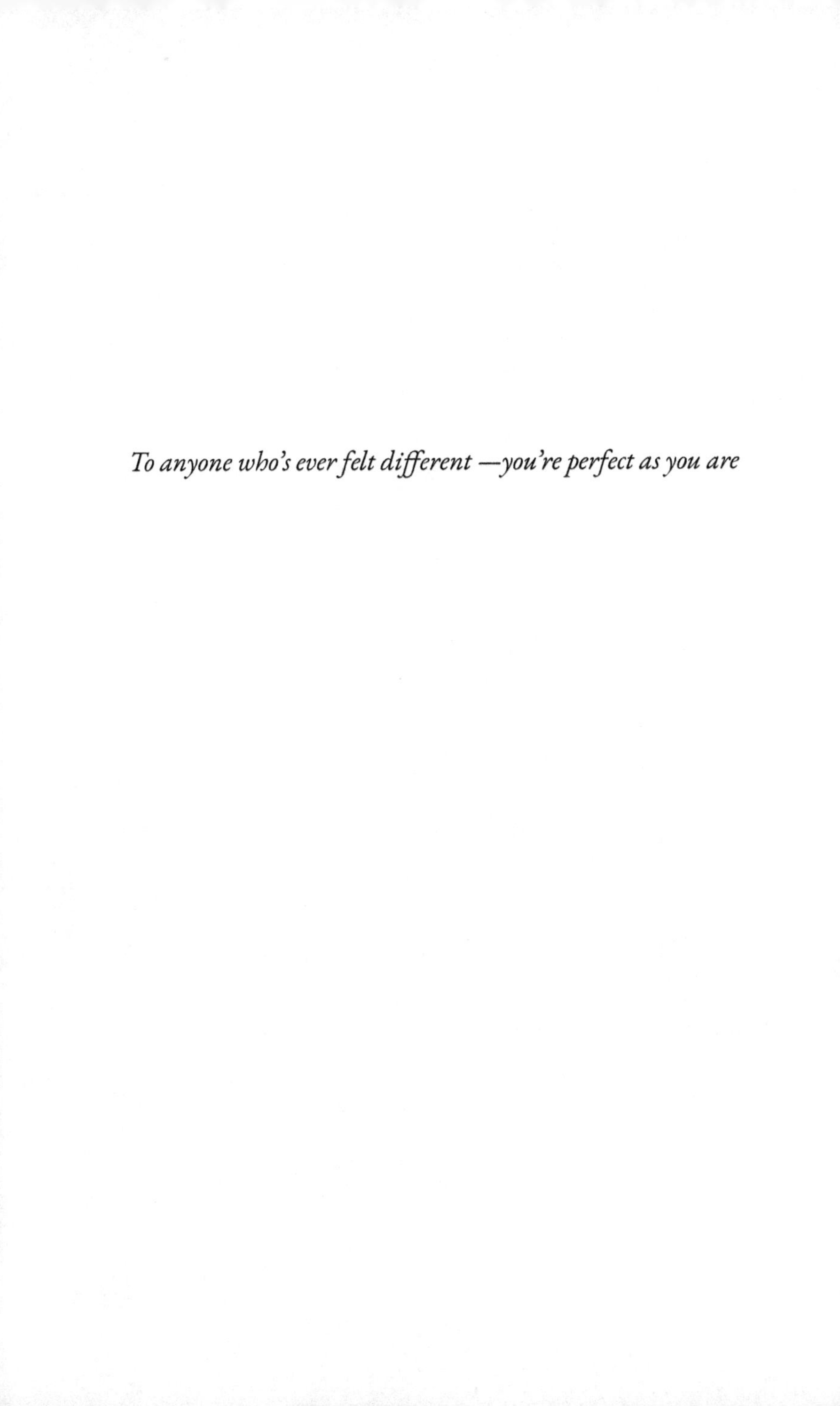

To anyone who's ever felt different —you're perfect as you are

STRIP BARE

SUN CITY #3

JADE CHURCH

CHAPTER ONE

"Jesus fucking Christ," Kit muttered as he nudged the door closed behind us. Aaron had made this stupid plan too easy. Why we had been dragged into this mess, I couldn't quite figure out—except, Ryan was our captain and Jamie was his girl. So messing with her meant messing with him and, by proxy, us.

Of course, technically Aaron was our captain too. co-captain, to be exact. But he was a shithead of epic proportions and I'd never liked him. So tenuous friendship with Jamie notwithstanding, I didn't exactly need an excuse to piss Aaron off and when Ryan had asked for our help...

I winced at the harshness of the bright light in the bathroom where Aaron had passed out. It was his place, so maybe he felt secure having his face against the toilet seat. It wasn't something I would do at the house I shared with Kit and Xander, my other teammates on the football team, and I was the one who did the majority of the cleaning.

I reached absently for the string of the big light and Kit gave me a wry look, making my hand halt in mid-air. It just felt *wrong* having it on at the best of times, let alone standing in the bathroom with Aaron and the remnants of what I had to assume was coke on the rim of the toilet. Classy to the last.

Kit sighed. "He's such a douche."

I couldn't disagree, nor could I hold back a smirk at the look of undisguised satisfaction on Kit's face as he leaned closer to Aaron with his phone out and snapped a photo. The flash went off, making the pop of Kit's blue hair seem ridiculously bright for a moment, and we both froze as we stared down at Aaron, waiting to see if he would stir.

Nothing.

"He's not dead, is he?" I wrinkled my nose as I stepped closer and nudged his leg with my foot. I wanted to help Jamie and Ryan out, but manslaughter wouldn't look too good on the record of a hopeful law graduate.

"S'goingon," Aaron slurred, trying to push himself upright and failing. Instead, he slid back against the wall, his head tucked down to his chest like it was too much effort to hold it up.

"Oh, *that* is a good one," Kit murmured and I snorted as he snapped a few more photos of Aaron with bloodshot blue eyes and a disgusting mixture of snot, coke, and blood around one nostril. Not that blackmail was any better than murder, really, on the legal side of things—but I would be steering clear of the actual threatening. At worst, I was an accessory-to-the-fact but I had plausible deniability going for me. Afterall, how was I, a concerned student, supposed to know that Kit was taking photos of our heavily intoxicated captain for evil purposes rather than good? All's fair in love and war, and Jamie really knew how to wage it.

Aaron snorted deeply and then coughed, spitting up what was probably a mixture of coke and phlegm into the toilet, and I tried not to gag.

Jamie really knew how to pick them. Of course, she was now with Ry and he was as nice as any guy got, usually. And it wasn't really her fault that Aaron had leaked her nudes across campus—though, the consequential revenge threesome had her signature stamped all over it. I shook my head. How had I wound up in this mess?

"Can we get out of here now?" I complained as Kit led us back through the door and down the stairs where the party was still raging after the final match of the season earlier that day. This was more Kit's scene than mine. Loud music and sweaty semi-strangers were not my idea of a good time. I would much rather be at home, digging into one of my new law textbooks—and yes, I knew how pathetic that probably sounded. Luckily, Kit didn't seem to mind. Sometimes he would stay on without me while I went home, but most times he came back with me.

It was probably the only time Kit left a party with a guy and *didn't* end the night by fucking him. Unfortunately.

Things between me and Kit were... complicated. Except, it was actually very simple. He was my friend. Probably the closest one I'd ever had considering how difficult I found it to connect with new people—it was the reason my mom was so pushy when it came to dating and any and all of my relationships. She was sweet, and I loved her, but her life didn't need to revolve around my love life—or lack thereof.

I liked Kit. More than liked, maybe. And sure, there had been a few moments where it had seemed like he might more-than-like me back. But it was hard to tell because Kit was naturally flirty. People gravitated toward him as we moved through the press of drunk students in the hall to the front door and I smiled tightly as more than one pair of sweaty palms tried to pull me closer to dance before I managed to escape. If Kit was sunshine, then I was frost—and it was only around him that I melted. People didn't instantly like me the way they did with him. It took them a while to warm up to me, and normally they only attempted it because I was part of the group.

Otherwise I would have continued on throughout my life at college the same way I had previously: looked over, ignored, or cautiously accepted but regarded as a little strange.

I was lucky to have Kit, really. For whatever reason, he'd pursued me after I'd joined the football team and it had given me someone else to talk to aside from my roommate. Maybe that was why I was scared to rock the boat with him. He'd been a permanent fixture in my life for several years now, I didn't want to lose him over likely-unrequited feelings that would probably fade with time.

"Leee-Oh," Kit dragged out my name as we breathed in the cool air and the sounds of the party faded behind us. I'd been so lost in my thoughts that I hadn't heard anything he'd had to say the last few minutes. "What are you thinking so hard about?" Kit cocked a dark eyebrow at me as we walked the few blocks between Ryan and Aaron's place to ours. It was still relatively early and the fading of the sunset cast interesting shades of pink into the baby blue strands of hair that Kit had re-dyed recently. He was so vibrant compared to my own pale skin and hair—the only color in my face came from my brown eyes. My mom said I looked like a true winter baby, and she wasn't wrong.

"I'm thinking I should dye my hair. Make it more interesting, like yours," I said easily, not wanting to get into the topic of my abysmal dating prospects—especially because Kit might offer to set me up and that would bum me out even more.

He tugged on the end of my semi-long hair and I fought off a shiver. "More interesting? You're kidding right?" I shrugged and he turned away so I couldn't work out his expression as he continued, "I don't think there's a way to improve perfection. I'm an artist, I should know."

I laughed and after a second he joined in, the sound warming me as we walked.

"Ryan is going to die when he sees these pics." Kit grinned as he held up his phone to show me and I winced. The flash had perfectly captured the bedraggled state Aaron had been in when we'd found him, making the reds of his rolling eyes more pronounced and the white of the coke still on his face harsher against the gray-tinge of his skin.

"He looks like a corpse."

"I know right," Kit said gleefully, pocketing his phone after putting the photos into the group chat we shared with Ryan and Xander. "Hopefully that cheers Jamie up."

Somehow, I doubted that a picture of her cheating ex off his face on drugs would make up for the fact that she'd been suspended from Radclyffe. The combination of academic probation thanks to a professor who had it out for her, and trumped up harassment charges from the best friend who'd been sleeping with Aaron, had pretty much only one outcome I had foreseen. Bryn, Kit's sister, and I had tried to run through what Jamie could say in her defense at the meeting with the advisors, but I hadn't been hopeful. Much like her brother, Bryn had been more optimistic about Jamie's chances. But then Jamie had sent a screenshot of the suspension letter she'd received via email to the group chat shortly after our football game and nobody had seen her since.

"Maybe," I murmured, and Kit sighed.

"You did everything you could to help her. It doesn't reflect on your badass lawyer-y skills, okay?"

I blinked at him before raising an eyebrow. "My *badass lawyer-y* skills?"

Kit grinned and it was lopsided, just the right amount of crooked to be adorable but his lips were just full enough to make the movement of his mouth sexy. "I said what I said." He stretched his arms up, curving his spine, and my mouth went dry at the quick glimpse of tanned, washboard abs beneath his tee.

"Fair enough," I croaked and then exhaled a quick breath as a familiar face approached. "Oh, look. You can show Ryan your photography skills in person."

Kit's face lit up as the dark-haired form of our football captain got closer. Ryan looked tired, and I couldn't blame him. I was glad Kit and Xander didn't want to host parties at our place all the time, I couldn't imagine anything worse.

"Hey man, did you see the photos in the group chat?"

Ryan perked up a little, brushing his hair off his face as he pulled his phone from the pocket of his jeans. "No, are they good?" Kit was practically bouncing as he watched for Ry's reaction, vibrating with a manic energy that would have set me on edge coming from anyone else. "Oh shit," Ryan said appreciatively, a grim smile forming on his face. "He's a fucking mess."

"Were you expecting anything less?" I said wryly and Ryan snorted.

"True." He ran his hands through his hair and it was rumpled enough that it didn't seem like the first time he'd done it. "God, I bet it's going to be an absolute shit-tip when I get back."

Kit clapped Ryan on the shoulder as we began to move past him. "Yep. Good luck with that."

"You can stay at ours?" I offered and felt a little guilty for how relieved I was when Ryan shook his head.

"Nah, it's okay. I'm heading to Nick's right now anyway."

"More scheming?" I raised an eyebrow and Kit grinned widely when Ryan nodded.

"Okay, well, good luck with that."

Ryan made his way past us in the opposite direction and we

were quiet as we continued walking home. I was almost sorry to leave the quiet evening air behind when we walked through the front door, but there was a peacefulness to our shared house that I appreciated.

I strode quickly into our kitchen for some water and relaxed at the sight of our open-plan kitchen-living room, it was probably my favorite thing about the house we all shared. It pained Kit, whose love language was color, but I loved the fact that everything gleamed in white, silver, and gray. It was modern and felt *clean*. I brushed invisible crumbs off of the white top of the breakfast bar and gulped back my drink as Kit followed me in and reached immediately for his laptop.

"Got work to do?"

Kit hummed and I hid my smile with my glass. Once he was absorbed in his work, there was pretty much no getting through to him.

"Okay, well I'm going to go study too."

No response. I laughed quietly as I set my glass in the sink and headed for the stairs. Compared to the kitchen, the rest of the house was more worn, not as recently renovated. But it was still nicer than Aaron and Ryan's place, even if they were slightly closer to campus than us. Of course, they also shared with Aaron's brother and his best friend—Brad and Cody. They were... fine, and also part of the football team. But I'd happily add another ten minutes onto our commute time than live with them, or Aaron.

My shoes were quiet against the carpet on the stairs and I quickly untied them and toed them off as I walked into my bedroom. Compared to the riot of color in Kit's room, mine seemed dull in comparison. I'd kept my walls bare and matched my sheets to the gray of the carpet, my desk was immaculate even though clothes were slung across the back of my chair, and my textbooks were organized by author, subject and then height.

Despite what I'd told Kit, I didn't move towards the textbooks or the laptop waiting on my desk. Instead, I pulled off my tee and unbuttoned my jeans before climbing onto my bed naked.

I let my hand travel down over my stomach, remembering the flash of skin Kit had offered me earlier as my hand moved lower. I'd been painfully hard for most of the night, making our pitstop at Aaron's party doubly uncomfortable. Normally I had more self-control, but it was hard to keep my cool after showering with Kit when our game was done. I tried not to look, I tried to ignore him, but he constantly called my attention back to him as he chattered on.

His blue hair had darkened to navy from the water and the muscles in his back had bunched together as he braced his hands against the wall, letting the water beat down and relax his body. My breath caught as a stab of desire hit me so fiercely my dick twitched in my hand. I tightened the fist around it, smoothing it up and down the shaft and curling around the sensitive head as I slowly increased my speed.

I had tried to stay focused, to get in and out of the shower as quickly as possible, but as much as other people may have been surprised to hear it—I was only human.

My hips thrust up as I imagined how differently that shower could have gone. If he'd finally kissed me, if my hands had fisted in his hair like stroking blue ink, the way our hands would have moved lower...

I gasped, my hips pushing my dick into my hand more firmly as I stroked my other hand down my abs, pretending they were his. My breaths became pants and my bed creaked a little as I reached the edge and grabbed for the tissue box I kept on my nightstand, just as my bedroom door flew open.

"Hey, I was just wondering—" Kit froze as he took me in, sprawled on my gray sheets with my dick in my hand, moments away from climax. "Shit," he said, but it sounded more like a growl and I could feel the heat in my cheeks growing when my dick twitched in response.

Kit's blue eyes darkened and he licked his lips before slowly reaching for the door handle. "I'm sorry. I'll knock next time."

I laughed, slightly breathless and he chuckled with me as I pulled a sheet over my lap and cleared my throat. There was a weird tension in the air and I blew out a small breath as I looked at him. Yeah, this was more awkward for me than him—how wouldn't it be when the object of my fantasy walked into my room *while* I fantasized? To Kit, this was nothing he probably hadn't already seen in the showers after a game, minus the hand on my dick.

"You needed something?"

Kit smirked and I knew what he was thinking, simply because he had a dirty mind and I knew him well after being at college together for nearly three years now. Clearly, I was the one who needed something—namely, the orgasm he'd interrupted. "I just wanted your opinion on a project I'm working on for class but, ah, it can wait."

"Good to know," I said dryly as I propped my arm behind my head and leaned back against my short, wooden headboard.

He snorted but nodded and I waited, thinking he had something else to say, but instead he just stood there.

"Was there something else?"

"What? Oh. No. I'll let you get back to..." Kit's eyes dropped to my lap and I tried not to react as I felt my dick twitch again. He smirked. "Well, you know. Have fun. Or something."

I rolled my eyes. "Goodbye, Kit."

"Try not to moan too loudly, some of us have to *actually* study."

I threw my pillow at him from behind my head and he laughed as it thumped against the closing door. I flopped back against the bed with a sigh. *Try not to moan too loudly.* Damn it. Now I felt weird finishing myself off, knowing that he knew what I was doing but not who I was thinking about.

A tingle spread through me as I dropped my hand to my dick, holding it idly as I considered. Or maybe... it was kind of hot.

My hand started to slowly move again and I bit back a groan. The problem was that this would only take the edge off. Kit was like an addiction I could never quite shake and wasn't so sure I wanted to quit.

With him in my mind, I let my eyes fall closed and my body take me back into oblivion.

CHAPTER TWO

"Class on a Sunday should be illegal," Bryn, Kit's sister, groaned as I highlighted the transcript in front of me. I hummed noncommittally and kept my eyes on the work we'd been assigned.

Truthfully, I didn't mind coming to class on the weekend. It was extra prep for the big exam we had coming up and while I was reasonably confident that I'd pass easily, I didn't want to get too cocky. I couldn't fail this exam. If I did, I wouldn't be able to continue on with the course next year—it wasn't something I'd ever really been concerned about. I was a good student. I was never late, I always went for extra credit on my assignments, I did far more than the expected level of background reading. And yet, now, at one of the most crucial points in my degree, I found myself more distracted than ever by blue hair and the richest laugh of anyone I'd ever met.

Of course, the fact that Kit had walked in on me thinking about him last night didn't help with my lack of focus today either.

"Leo?" Bryn said and I jolted, looking up into a pair of blue eyes that were a disconcertingly similar shade to her brother's. "I asked if I could look at your notes for the Jefferson case study."

"Right. Yes. Of course." I slid them over to her and pretended I didn't see the slight narrowing of her eyes as she tucked a strand of long blonde hair behind her ear. I could feel her stare burning into the side of my face the longer I avoided her eyes, so finally I heaved a sign and looked at her. "What?"

Bryn's lip twitched, fighting off a smile, and I realized I'd probably sounded too cold, so I tried for a smile while I waited for her to spit out whatever was bothering her. "You seem like your head is elsewhere today."

I rolled my eyes and turned back to my notes as the hum of quiet chatter seemed to swell and our professor made the rounds. "My head is firmly attached to my shoulders, thanks."

"You're being pedantic."

"You're being annoying."

Bryn laughed, the sound high and curling and I let a reluctant smile take over. Since she'd transferred to Sun City from California, Bryn had taken to me pretty quickly, almost like I was just another brother to her. "So what's on your mind?"

I hesitated, my highlighter pen just a few scant inches from the paper in front of me. I decided I'd give her a half-truth, figuring she wouldn't really want to hear about me lusting over her brother. "Just tired and thinking about last night—Kit and I did a favor for Ryan."

"Oh?"

Bryn turned back to her textbook and I slid her my case study notes, complete with color-coded tabs, and she eyed it appreciatively as I winced. "Don't mess up my system." Her eyebrow raise spoke volumes and I shrugged, unrepentant. "It was actually a favor for Jamie, technically."

"Ryan's new girlfriend?"

"Yeah…"

"What was the favor?"

I opened my mouth and then shut it again. If I told her what we'd done, would that make her culpable too? Her blue eyes flashed when I took too long to answer and I relented. "We took photos of Aaron coked up out of his mind and then Kit and I showed them to coach this morning."

Bryn choked on the water she'd sipped from her bottle and I pretended not to notice, turning back to my work. "I can't decide if I'm alarmed or impressed."

"Why not both?"

She snorted in agreement and we went back to working quietly together, but my brain still swirled alarmingly. I'd hoped that studying would be the perfect distraction from thinking about Kit and what he'd caught me doing—but if anything, the quiet and my brain's ability to multitask proved to pull Kit's face to the forefront of my mind. The spark and surprise on his face when he'd opened the door, the huskiness to his voice that I'd replayed a *lot* as I picked up where I'd left off before he'd interrupted.

I needed to get it together. Kit and I were never going to happen, and if I didn't focus on what was actually important now I'd end up flunking out of my degree and everything I'd worked for. I wouldn't let that happen.

Shoving any thoughts of Kit to the side, I packed up my notes and smiled when Bryn looked at me in question.

I needed to move, to work out some of my frustration, and with any luck Xander might be in the basketball courts right about now. I didn't particularly care about sports, I'd joined the football team to make friends and because it was good exercise, not with any grand notions about going pro. If I was being honest, I actually preferred our regular basketball matches to our football games, mostly because the stakes were lower and there wasn't anyone gaping at us from the sidelines.

The courts weren't too far from campus and I was relieved to see Xander there, shooting baskets. One thing I liked about Xander was that he was easygoing. He wouldn't ask me what was wrong—because something had to be for me to deviate from my routine—we would just play.

Predictably, we did just that. It wasn't until we agreed that the sunshine was becoming a bit much to play in, especially for my paler complexion, that he asked if I wanted to talk about anything. The concern in his dark eyes was clear, but the relaxed set of his shoulders told me he wouldn't mind if I declined and I appreciated it.

Xander was kind of like a puppy. Or maybe a rottweiler. He was tall and broad and his sharp cheekbones and jawline made him seem intimidating, but he was all bark and no bite. A softie at heart.

"I'm just going to head home and shower," I said and he nodded easily.

"Yeah, might want to make it a cold one, you're looking kinda pink."

I grimaced. "Great."

His lip twitched and I flipped him off as we walked out of the courts while he tied his long hair back into a bun. "Have you seen Kit?"

My heart felt like it stuttered at his name. "Not since this morning."

"Ah yeah, I heard about that. I saw coach in his office earlier and he was still raging."

I almost felt sorry for Aaron. Almost. Coach's wrath was legendary and I wouldn't want to be caught on the other end of it.

"Anyway, I think he was looking for you."

"Coach?"

"Kit," Xander said with a roll of his eyes and I didn't even comment, my mouth filling with saliva as queasiness washed over me. It was ridiculous to have that reaction, this was Kit. My best friend. He probably just wanted help studying or needed me to read one of his essays. There was no way he wanted to talk about last night. Was there?

The Box was a regular haunt for our little group and, despite its popularity, I felt strangely comfortable there. Too many places looked the same nowadays and they all tended to use the overly bright lighting and 'natural' fake aesthetic that gave me a headache.

The Box wasn't like that though. During the day, the lights were a faint, barely-there pink. As the day wore on, the color deepened until the lights were a deep red by the time the bar closed. Another thing I appreciated was that *The Box* didn't try and appear as anything but what it was—a little quirky, a little cheesy, commercial but fun. We had a regular booth along the left wall, but there were plenty of small tables too that sat in front of the small stage that Jamie often performed on. If I was being honest, open mic night was probably my least favorite time to come to the bar so, whenever possible, I ignored the Wednesday-night invites.

They'd recently installed a new, cheesy sign framed above the seats of the booth diagonally opposite ours and my eyes kept straying back to it when I got bored of the conversation. It read: *One tequila, two tequila, three tequila, floor.* Something about it amused me more than it really warranted, and more than once Kit had looked over and smiled when he saw me mouthing the words of the picture as I re-read it. He'd given no indication that he'd been searching for me earlier that day and I wasn't sure if I was relieved or disappointed about that. Maybe he just wanted to completely forget what had happened, put it behind us. Probably wise.

Jamie and Liv, her roommate, had been the last to arrive and that was pretty typical—Liv was as punctual as me, but Jamie couldn't get somewhere on time if she had a watch stapled to her forehead. I supposed that was a quirk Ryan found endearing. Or maybe it was Jamie's whole *thing*—she gave off very clear *don't fuck with me* vibes that was in complete contrast to Liv, who tended to be on the shyer side, and could easily have doubled as a ballerina with her slight build and long, bronzed legs. If I wasn't so clearly playing for the other team, maybe I could appreciate whatever it was that had Ryan so obsessed and Xander moony-eyed. It was particularly unfortunate for Xander though, as Liv was more interested in Jamie than any guy in the booth.

Kit's smile was smug as he tucked his phone back into his pocket after showing Jamie the photo of Aaron passed out, coke smeared all over him. The delight on her face was almost comical considering how disgusting the photo was, you would have thought she'd been looking at puppies or something. Nick, Jamie's coursemate, and Ryan's scheming had paid off and they'd managed to speak to the Dean and get her suspension revoked. While I was happy for her, I was finding it a little hard to concentrate on the positives.

Nick was a nice guy. Smart, friendly... ridiculously attractive with his dark skin and cutting cheekbones, and I *knew* he'd slept with Kit at least once. I tried to be nice or, at least, not openly hostile, but when Kit looked at me with a raised eyebrow I knew I hadn't succeeded.

I released a breath slowly and let my shoulders relax as Nick leaned in to Kit and said something quietly, making him laugh and my body tense up again. I was relieved when Jamie and Ryan stood and said their goodbyes before leaving, because if they were going it meant that *we* could go too. Only, Kit didn't look like he was in a rush to move.

My eye caught Kat's green pair and I looked away quickly. She was friends with Jamie and worked at the box and the first time we'd met she'd made it very clear she was interested in me. Awkward. I didn't exactly have a sign around my neck that screamed *GAY* but still, I'd felt kind of embarrassed for her when she'd come out of the restroom at the box that night with her shirt unbuttoned a lot further than it had been when she'd gone in.

Kat was... precocious, though, and as Liv slid out of the booth with a casual wave of one golden hand and Nick and Kit continued to chatter on, I knew that meant she would soon be turning to me for conversation.

I looked quickly to Kit, cutting Nick off mid-word as I stood. "Don't you have a shift soon?"

Kit checked the time on his phone and sighed. "Yeah. I guess we should go."

"Oh, I'm heading that way anyway," Nick said cheerfully and I tried not to scowl at his stupidly handsome face.

"Oh," Kat said as she looked between the three of us, a hint of color rising to her creamy cheeks. "Right. Well, I guess I'll head home then."

I nearly winced. I wasn't the most perceptive of people, but even I could tell that she felt like she'd been ditched. "You could come to *Cocoa & Rum* too? I'm going to study there while Kit does his shift."

She smiled slightly, her dimples flashing. "That's alright, but thanks. I have a paper to write anyway and I need to talk to

Billy about one of my shifts next week. Catch up with you later?"

We nodded as she made her way behind the bar to talk to a short, skinny guy that I could only assume was her manager. One of the best things about Kit was that he was chatty, so I knew I wouldn't have to do much to hold up a conversation between me and Nick on the way to the coffee shop where Kit worked. Though, it was just about late enough in the day that *Cocoa & Rum* had likely transitioned into its evening wine-bar menu but it would probably still be quiet for a few more hours at least. It wasn't really clear to me why Kit bothered to work there, other than that he must like it, because he and Bryn weren't exactly strangers to money. His parents probably had more in their bank accounts than mine would earn in a lifetime, but both Kit and his sister were surprisingly down-to-earth.

The late afternoon, early-evening air was refreshingly cool after the heat inside *The Box* and the sun was still shining weakly as the night rapidly approached. It was only a short walk to the coffee shop and our long legs ate up the distance quickly. I nodded to Nick as he continued on past *Cocoa & Rum* and headed in the direction of campus through the park.

Kit raised an eyebrow at me as he pulled open the glass door. "You could at least pretend to like him, you know."

I blinked. "I don't dislike him." I caught the door as we moved inside and the smell of coffee beans hit me. It was a strong scent, but I found it soothing now because it was how Kit always smelled when he got home from a shift. "We just don't have much in common."

"How would you know? You've barely spoken to him."

"Why does it matter so much to you?" I said curiously, but clearly with more ice in my voice than I meant to project because Kit sighed, scrubbing a hand across his face as we hovered by the large counter he would be standing behind later as he served drinks and took orders.

"Because you push people away without realizing it. I just think you should give him—and yourself—a chance."

I nodded slowly. "Okay." I pointed to a table in the corner of the room that looked quiet and faced the large glass windows so that I could watch the park opposite when I wasn't studying. "I'll be over there. Have a good shift."

"You don't have to stay—"

"It's good for me to get out of the house," I said carefully and he half-smiled at that. This had become our routine, and he knew how much I liked to maintain those once I got into a habit.

"Make sure you take a break," he said as he headed towards a door behind the counter that read *staff only* and I couldn't hold back a smile as I sat down at the table I'd indicated. I didn't always stay here for Kit's shifts, but he often worked at least one late shift on the weekend so I grabbed a textbook or my laptop to read case files and sat in the ambience while we both worked.

There was a new guy behind the counter that I hadn't seen before and he gave me a slow smile and nod when he noticed my eyes on him. His hair was a sandy blonde that was warmer than my own and he smiled at Kit with more than a little flirtatiousness when he joined him by the register. *Great.* We'd just got rid of Nick, and now here was a brand new proverbial version to take his place in a flirt-a-thon.

I tilted my body away from the counter and bit my lip in irritation when I tried to continue watching them out of the corner of my eye—I was jealous, and I knew it. Knew I had no right to be, especially as Kit didn't really seem to be treating his colleague any differently than anyone else he might talk to. I mean, I wouldn't have minded if his smile had been about ten-percent less warm, or his laugh just a little more forced. I tried to focus on the court transcripts in front of me, tucked into the textbook I had brought with me as an example of whatever the page was talking about. I wouldn't know, because my attention was firmly caught in the grasp of Kit, laughing, joking, smiling at this *guy* I'd heard nothing about. No. I needed to focus.

A glass hit my table with a thunk and I jumped a little, too busy pretending to read to have seen Kit head in my direction.

"Thanks," I muttered as I took a sip of what turned out to be a very tangy beer. I tried not to grimace and Kit laughed.

"I take it this one isn't good?"

"It's... an acquired taste."

For whatever reason, Kit delighted in getting me to try new drinks every time I was in here—getting me to branch out, push myself or whatever.

"Who's the new guy?" I asked, trying to keep my tone nonchalant.

"Funny," Kit said, mouth twisting like he'd tasted something sour before the expression smoothed out, "he just asked me the same thing about you. His name's Harley. He just started last week." Kit paused, like he was considering something before he continued, "Why? You interested?"

My brow furrowed as I shrank back. "What? No."

Kit's mouth eased into a smile and I felt a little dazed at the close proximity of it. "Okay. Well, good."

Good? What did that mean? Did he not want me to be interested in other guys? Or did he just think Harley was an ass? The words couldn't quite make their way out of my mouth and by the time I'd had another sip of the thick beer, he'd already left to serve a new batch of customers.

I focused on the table in front of me, trying not to read into the words or search for hidden meanings, but it was hard because I really had no idea what he'd meant.

"You look like you need rescuing," a warm, deep voice said and I looked up sharply. Clear, blue-gray eyes met mine and I tried to keep the confusion off my face as Harley set down a drink in a tall glass next to me with one sun-tanned hand.

"What?"

"The beer." He nodded to the drink Kit had brought me and then smiled. I couldn't help but fixate on how straight his teeth were and had to force myself to look away at the drink he'd set down.

"Oh. Yeah it's a tradition we have."

Something sparked in his eyes and I leaned forward slightly, curious, like I could work out what it meant if I just peered a little closer.

"So is it only Kit who can buy you a drink then? Or are you open to... other drinks?"

I blinked. *What the hell was he talking about?* Thankfully I was saved from having to decode whatever Harley had meant by the appearance of Kit behind his shoulder.

Kit's eyes found the new drink on the table immediately and his eyebrows furrowed. "What's that?"

"A drink," Harley said, mouth quirking up into a half-smile before he nodded at me. "Try it."

"He already has a drink."

"It didn't seem like he was enjoying it very much." Harley leaned slightly closer to Kit as he spoke, a strange friction rising between them as I watched, baffled by what was happening and why they cared so much about what drink I had. I reached for the glass Harley brought me and sipped at the thick red drink. Tangy but sweet, with a crunch that was oddly satisfying, I hummed in appreciation as I opened my eyes and found both of them watching me.

"It's good. What is it?"

Kit's mouth turned down and I felt like I'd somehow

disappointed him, but what was I supposed to do? Lie? The beer was awful and Harley's drink was a lot nicer, even if the burn of alcohol did ruin it slightly.

"Fresh watermelon daiquiri," Harley said, leaning one hand down against the table as he reached for my glass and took a long swallow. His throat working was strangely hypnotic and he grinned at me as he placed my drink back onto the table before throwing a glance at Kit, and I didn't know what to say next.

"Customers," Kit said abruptly as a group of three people walked in and I looked at them in a daze before my eyes flew wide.

I stood abruptly and Harley backed up, eyebrows high as he headed back behind the counter.

This could not be happening. Shit. I looked at Kit, my heart hammering so hard I could feel the skin of my chest vibrating. I gripped my hands tightly together, the nails digging in and yet I was still asleep. I had to be dreaming. Because otherwise, I was about to become royally screwed.

CHAPTER THREE

I WAS EXPERIENCING ONE OF THOSE CHEESY RECORD rip moments that happened in movies. Only, this was my real life, and I was freaking out. Somehow, my parents and my baby sister were walking through the door of *Cocoa & Rum* and looking around expectantly. *Shit, shit, shit.*

There weren't very many options for me now. I either had to own up to what I'd done and probably disappoint a lot of people, as well as breaking some trust, or I had to potentially wreck the best friendship I'd ever had. How the hell had they found me here?

My phone vibrated in my pocket and I fished it out in a daze as my mom's eyes scanned the space around us, looking for me. There was a text on the screen and I swallowed down my curse as I read it and looked up to see my sister staring directly at me.

It simply read: *Surprise!* With a rolling eyes emoji and a screenshot of the family-friend location sharing app.

I grabbed Kit's arm as he spotted my family and made to wave, but it was too late. My mom's round face lit up as she noticed Kit's sharp movement and saw me standing next to him.

"Kit," I said urgently and his eyes focused on mine immediately. "Fuck."

"What's wrong?"

My family were getting closer, just a few tables away, waving and calling my name and I felt dizzy. My face was getting hotter, burning in my cheeks, and I was breathing hard like I'd just run a marathon. Normally the spectacle alone would have had me groaning, but the panic washing through me was more pressing. I could either risk disappointing my family, or I could risk ruining my friendship with Kit. Either way, I was fucked.

My dad was close enough that I could see the wrinkles in his tee, probably from the drive down, and I didn't know what I was going to tell them. My heart felt like it was in my throat, a vague nausea working its way through my body as a cold sweat slipped over my skin. If Kit was really my friend, he'd understand. Or at the very least, hopefully he'd forgive me.

"Just go with it," I gasped as I stepped into Kit's warmth and closed my mouth over his. His lips parted on a gasp and I took advantage, kissing him deeper, and then pulling away as I heard a squeal. Kit looked dizzy and I wished it was from my kiss instead of shock, but I didn't have time to comfort him right then. Not with three bodies now crowding around us.

"Hi Mom," I said, stepping away from Kit as she flung her arms around me and engulfed me in the comforting smell of lavender. "What are you doing here?"

"Surprise," Saylor said, mimicking her text in the most deadpan voice she could manage and I bit back my smile as my dad nudged her.

"Well we wanted to show your sister around the campus, and of course I wanted to visit my boy." She pulled away to study my face, her brown eyes the mirror of my own, and despite everything I felt some of the tension leave my body. Then she turned to Kit.

"And you must be Kit! Leo's boyfriend."

Fuck.

I looked anxiously at Kit, but he didn't look like he'd even heard what my mother had said, still dazed from the previous contact of our lips. I couldn't blame him. If it wasn't for my ability to rigidly compartmentalize everything in my life, I would probably be falling apart over the fact that I had just kissed one of the only real, true friends I'd ever had. I could only hope I hadn't fucked things up permanently between us.

"You should have called," I tried to say gently, but knew my tone must have been off by the way my mom's mouth turned down at the corners. "I mean," I scrambled, trying to recover, "that I have exams coming up and I don't know how much time I'll get to spend with you."

Her smile returned and I let out a breath of relief. "Oh, don't worry about that darling. We won't get in the way of your studying. Now, it's been a long day—how about you show us to your place? I'm not sure I remember how to get there."

I glanced quickly at Kit and then sharply away again when I found him watching me. "Um, sure. Let me just get my stuff."

"What about your—"

I cut her off, not wanting her to repeat the words I knew had probably screwed everything over already. "Kit has to finish his shift."

"No," KIt said roughly and I froze part-way through packing away my notes. "Harley can cover for me."

"I thought he was new." I tried to keep the alarm out of my voice and knew to most people, they never would have noticed anything amiss. But Kit was not most people. "Surely you need to stay and—"

"Nope," he repeated, popping the letters with force, and my mouth went so dry all I could do was nod.

My mom beamed as she wrapped me in another hug, making me crumple the notes sticking out of the textbook as it was crushed to my chest awkwardly. "Excellent. I can't wait to spend some time with you both."

I didn't bother to reply, just nodded at Harley as he watched the group of us file out of *Cocoa & Rum* with something like disappointment on his face. I gave him an apologetic smile but couldn't maintain it when I glanced behind me and found Kit following close behind, blue eyes burning into my back.

"Kit," I murmured as we headed into the park but he shook his head, jaw tight. It was rare that he looked serious, normally so quick to smile.

"Later."

Dread pooled in the bottom of my stomach. I'd never had a fight with Kit before, had never really seen him angry at all. I had no idea what to expect from him and that made me more nervous than anything else.

The streetlights in the park had come on in the short time I'd sat in the bar and their warm glow made everything feel cheery despite the anxiety that churned inside me. I wasn't hugely in touch with my emotions, but even I could tell that what I was feeling was a dose of worry, confusion, and shame about lying to my parents and putting Kit in this position. But there was also a part of me caught up in the memory of Kit's mouth, the way he'd tasted and the way he'd gasped like he'd felt just as electrified as me. That was unlikely though, a fantasy spinning out only in my head. In reality, it was probably the shock that had him gasping into my mouth like he'd die if he didn't get to taste me.

My dad ducked his tall frame under a low-hanging branch

as we walked down the off-shoot of the main pathway and the familiar gesture soothed some of my panic. This was my *family*. They had always supported me. Sure, they might be a little upset or disappointed, but I'd thought it was a little white lie. I should have known it would come back to bite me in the ass.

People still milled about, the perks of a student dominated city, so despite the dark everything still felt very much alive. My mom was chattering on at Kit and under normal circumstances I would have been amused for him to meet someone who talked more than him, but now it only made me nervous about what they might be saying.

I should just tell them that I'd lied. Rip the band-aid off. But when Kit looked back at me, his eyes appearing almost black in the low-light, the words dried up on my tongue. It was selfish, but I couldn't help wondering *what if this is all I get of him?* What if this small taste was all I could have? So instead, I swallowed my confession. At least, until I could speak to Kit.

"Where are you guys staying?" I asked my dad and he blinked, brushing a strand of hair as light as my own out of his face.

"Is that not where we're going?"

"What?"

"Well, we just thought we'd stay with you, darling." My mom said, eyes bright as she beamed at me. "You can share with Kit for a few days, right? Saylor can take the sofa and your dad and I will share your room."

"Right," I said faintly. Because what else could I say? Of course it wouldn't be a problem for me to share a bed with my boyfriend. Fuck, this was spiralling out of control. Sure, Kit had the biggest room in the house, but I couldn't just share his space, his *bed*. It wasn't fair to him. None of this was his fault. I needed to come clean. Now. "Mom, actually I—"

"Sounds like a plan," Kit interrupted and I choked on my own spit. "Leo and I are happy to share."

Saylor shot me a look and I fought back a grimace. She was two years younger than me and we'd always been relatively close, even if I was terrible at keeping in touch with her. In fact, most people assumed we were twins when they saw us together and it wasn't an unreasonable assumption to make—her hair was a slightly lighter shade of white-blonde than my own but her eyes were dark just like my mom's. In the dark, she nearly glowed and I wondered if I looked the same to anyone else passing by.

We rounded a corner and ended up on the west-side exit of the park, just a few blocks from our place. I looked automatically to our left as we walked, my eyes taking in Ryan and Aaron's house opposite the large line of trees. It was force of habit, nothing more, but my dad looked at it expectantly and turned in that direction before I caught his arm.

"That's where our co-captain's are," Kit said. "We're not too much further away."

"That's nice," my mom murmured and we walked the last part of the way home in near-silence.

A warm hand brushed my own and I jolted, looking up at Kit in confusion as his fingers slid between mine and squeezed once before letting go. Was that his way of saying he understood? That he wasn't mad? I curled my fingers inwards, annoyed at the way they still tingled from his touch as we shepherded my family through our front door. They chatted amongst themselves as they kicked off their shoes and my heart seemed to speed up as I raised my eyes to find Kit watching me, an unreadable expression on his face.

Xander walked out of his room shirtless and leaned over the railing at the top of the stairs as we filed past into the kitchen. "Guests?"

"Surprise visitors," I said with a wince and then scowled at the way my sister was smiling at him. "Go put on a shirt."

He smirked and Saylor raised an eyebrow at me.

"He's too old for you," I protested and she snorted.

"I'm an adult, Leo. I can make my own decisions."

"Sure." I rolled my eyes. "Come back to me when you're legally allowed to drink."

Her eyes flashed and I smothered a grin. It was a sore spot for her because she was born early enough to be the oldest one in any classes she'd taken, but just too late to join the next year group.

"So you're thinking about college?" I said to her, trying to keep the peace as I handed out water and soda to her and my parents.

"Maybe." She shrugged. "I just finished my intern year, so I have to decide what I want to do next."

"Well, Radclyffe has a lot to offer," Xander said with a smirk as he walked into the kitchen and sat down at the breakfast bar. At least he'd put on a shirt.

"Noted," Saylor replied and I scowled at my roommate. My parents were big on real-life experience, so we'd both waited a year before going to college where we'd worked or interned for a company to get experience before deciding whether to pursue a degree. I'd interned at a small-town law firm for the summer before I started classes and loved every second of it.

"You don't mind if I steal him for a moment do you?" Kit said, his voice startling close to my ear as he smiled at my parents. I was probably the only one who noticed the strained edge to it and I felt a little queasy as my mom nodded and smiled. "We need to get your room ready," Kit said in explanation but I knew that wasn't the real reason he was pulling me away.

I followed him up to his room begrudgingly, my body

tensing more and more the closer we got to the landing, until his door closed behind us and I braced myself.

It was quiet for a moment as Kit paced in front of his desk. It was a mess of art supplies and books that I knew looked too disorganized to me but probably made sense to him. I had no doubt that he knew where everything in that pile was.

"Kit—" I tried and he shook his head. "I'm sorry," I said anyway. "I can go downstairs right now and tell them that I lied."

He shook his head and I lingered by the closed door, unsure what he wanted from me. "What would that help?"

"Um, you?" I offered and he stopped moving to stare at me, his blue hair mussed from running his hands through it.

"Tell me," he said and I knew what he was asking.

"I told her we were together so she'd stop trying to set me up with people. She somehow got this one guy to approach me at *Cocoa & Rum* recently for a blind date she'd set-up without me knowing. It was the most painful experience I think I've ever had. So I told her I was seeing someone to get her to stop."

Kit was nodding and I tried to breathe out slowly, calmly, but it was hard when I felt like our friendship was on the line here. No matter what I felt for him, I wouldn't risk what we had.

"I thought it would be a little white lie, I swear I never expected them to show up like this."

He nodded again and I wanted to shake him.

"Can you please say something?"

"I'm thinking."

I wanted to snap at him, to ask why he couldn't think aloud, but I wasn't really in a position to be demanding anything.

"Okay," he said eventually, sitting down on the edge of his bed and tugging on a loose navy thread from the comforter.

"Okay?" I repeated disbelievingly. "What does that mean?"

"It means I'm mad you didn't tell me about this at the time so I could be a little more prepared, and I'm mad that the only explanation you gave me was *just go with it*. But," he said, letting out a heavy breath as he slumped backward, revealing a small stretch of his taut stomach beneath his tee. "I understand why you did it and I'll get over the other stuff."

That shouldn't have hurt. I knew the kiss hadn't meant anything to him, but it was different hearing him say it. "I'll come clean to them."

"No."

My face fell slack as I stared at him. "I really need you to tell me what's going on in your head."

He shrugged. "If you come clean, she'll go right back to setting you up on unwanted dates." A dark look passed across his face, slanting his eyebrows down as his tongue played with his lip piercing. "So don't tell them. We'll just have to pretend."

"Pretend to... want you?"

"Pretend you have me."

I swallowed and wasn't sure when we'd moved closer together. "You really don't have to do this."

"Maybe I want to," he said quietly and my heart raced as he looked up at me from his low vantage point on the bed. "I wouldn't be a very good friend otherwise, right?"

Friend. I forced a smile. "Right."

"Then let's do this." He held out his hand and I took it, pulling him up from the bed until our chests were flush before I stepped back. This was a terrible fucking idea. The worst form of torture, a small glimpse of what I was missing with him. But Kit was right—if I confessed to my mother, her meddling would start up all over again and probably with more urgency than before when she realized I'd lied.

"Let's do this," I agreed reluctantly and then caught his arm as moved past me for the door. "Thank you."

"For what?"

"Not yelling. I was expecting you to be... Well, just thank you. For understanding."

We were standing closer than I realized and his breath feathered lightly across my lips as I looked into his eyes. There was a softness there that was usually covered by quick humor and mischief but I loved that he let me see it. Unguarded.

"I would never yell at you. Ever."

For some reason the words brought a lump to my throat so I just nodded in response and then jumped when a light knock sounded on the door behind me.

"Hey," Saylor said as she pushed it open without invitation. "Mom wanted me to come up and check you two weren't getting *distracted*." She rolled her eyes and I frowned as Kit took a small step back from me.

"And what if we were? You thought bursting in here was the best thing to do?"

"Please." She snorted as she waved between us. "This is so not happening. You may have Mom convinced, but I'm not buying it."

I folded my arms across my chest as I stared into eyes infuriatingly similar to my own. "You're wrong." Maybe it didn't matter if she knew, but if I couldn't convince my kid sister that Kit was mine then how were we supposed to fool anyone else?

"I've seen more chemistry between inanimate objects than you two."

Kit laughed, long and slow, and it made my stomach swoop strangely, like I'd just approached the drop on a rollercoaster and found myself unexpectedly falling. "How's this for chemistry?"

He closed the distance between us and slid one of his large hands over my jaw before fisting it in my hair and tugging my mouth to his. He tasted like whatever fruity beer he'd sampled on his shift and a sweetness that was wholly him. His tongue met mine in a slow guide as he pulled away, nipping at my bottom lip before whispering in my ear tauntingly—"Just go with it."

I was breathing hard and trying to disguise it and couldn't tell whether he was affected too. There was a slight smirk on his lips that had the blood in my head rushing further south and it wasn't until my sister cleared her throat that I remembered she was still standing there.

"I can admit when I'm wrong." She studied my face for a second before turning around and walking out of the room, calling her behind her as she went. "I'm going out for dinner with Xander tomorrow by the way."

"What?" I made to follow her, anything to distract me from the lingering after effects of Kit's kiss. "He didn't say anything to me about it," I muttered to Kit. "Aren't there like, courtesy rules for that kind of thing?"

"That's a little..."

I sighed. "I didn't mean it like that. He's my friend. She's my sister. My *baby* sister. Shouldn't he check I'm cool with this? For the sake of friendship?"

Kit shrugged as he closed his door behind us and I turned away to watch Saylor sashay into the kitchen. I loved her, but the girl was trouble. "They're both adults, Leo."

I grimaced. He wasn't wrong.

"So Xander," Saylor said as we walked into the room. "About dinner tomorrow night—"

"What dinner?" Xander looked at me with wide eyes, genuinely clueless, and I snorted in disbelief. Fucking Saylor.

"The one you're going to take me to."

"I—um, yeah. Sure." He looked to me again and I shrugged. The truth was, Xander was a nice guy and Kit was right. They *were* both adults.

"There's my two lovebirds," my mom cooed as she stood from our couch and pecked me on the cheek. "I've missed you," she said quietly and I smiled as I hugged her.

"I missed you too." And it was true. As overbearing as she could be, it was good to see her. "How long are you guys thinking of staying?"

"Maybe til next weekend, it depends on how your sister finds the campus. She might want to join in on some of the taster sessions."

Crap. Almost a whole week of sharing a bed with Kit.

"Well, I mean Saylor could always stay longer if you guys need to head back," I said, twisting my hands together behind my back and feeling grateful when Xander chipped in.

"I could drive you," he suggested with a quick glance at my sister and then me.

My dad grinned. "Nonsense, Leo doesn't mind sharing with his boyfriend."

Xander raised an eyebrow and I interrupted before he could say anything. "Yeah of course, but Saylor might want to look around herself. Spend some time here without you guys."

"Of course." My mom nodded as she stepped back and took my dad's hand. "That makes sense. Well, we'll just see how we go.

I led them upstairs while Kit grabbed some bedding for Saylor to use on the couch and I tried not to think about sharing a bed with him. Waking up with him. Especially after kissing him. Twice.

Once my parents were settled in my room, I walked hesitantly into Kit's and stared at the bed until he walked into the room behind me.

"I don't bite." When I didn't laugh, he sighed. "Leo, we're friends. This is fine, okay? But if it makes you feel better I can sleep on the floor."

"No," I said quickly. "It's fine. You're right. Let's just go to sleep, it's been a long day.

"Sure." Kit unzipped his jeans and the sound of the zipper had heat rising to my cheeks. I undressed quickly and then climbed into his bed sans shirt, but wearing my PJ bottoms. This was fine. I could do this.

The light vanished and Kit got into bed on the other side of me, the weight of his body next to mine an unfamiliar, but not unwelcome, presence.

"Goodnight, Leo."

"Goodnight." I tried to keep the breathlessness from my voice as I battled down the naked want I was feeling, but it was hard. Something about the darkness made his proximity feel electric, like I could reach out and touch him and find him on the exact same page as me. Wanting what I wanted. Craving me the way I craved him. That was what was so dangerous about this situation, sharing his bed, it made him feel accessible. Like he wasn't just mine for a moment, but could be mine forever and I wasn't sure if that would ruin me.

As the night settled around us and I attempted to sink into sleep, I could only hope that my heart survived this mess intact.

CHAPTER FOUR

Waking up with Kit was, unfortunately, something I could get used to and would undoubtedly miss once my parents left. I had hoped the reality of morning breath, snoring, and cover hogging might help make this feel less... right. But, annoyingly enough, Kit in the morning was just adorable. And so I knew I needed to call in reinforcements when my mom insisted on the both of us showing them and Saylor around campus and the city. Kit blinked at the sight of his sister waiting outside our door for us and I avoided his eyes as I hustled everyone out and toward the green.

"So, this park runs through the center of town and depending on where you're headed you can choose which trail to follow." I pointed to the center of the converging pathways up ahead, marked by a large statue so weathered I had no idea what it was supposed to be. "So if you head that way," I pointed to the left, "you'll find yourself at the main campus entrance. If you continue straight ahead you'll be closer to the bar we were at yesterday and the other restaurants aren't too far from there."

My mom was nodding seriously like this was vital information while Saylor scrolled on her phone.

"Over to the right leads to the mall and out of town if you go far enough," Bryn cut in and I was relieved to not be the only one talking. We were on the same course and the fact that she was also Kit's sister had made Bryn an easy friend to make. "There's also the sports stadium down that way too."

"That's where you both play?" my dad said, perking up as he looked at me and Kit.

I nodded but it was Kit who replied. "Yeah, I'd say you should come and watch a game but we haven't got any more real matches lined up now until next season. We had our last game a couple nights ago."

"Another time," my mom said and I couldn't help my wince —were we going to have to pretend Kit and I were together every time she visited?

"What are you hoping to study?" Bryn asked my sister, brushing a strand of her long blonde hair out of eyes. I suspected Kit was naturally blonde too but I'd never seen him with his roots showing and his brows were dark.

"I'm not sure I *am* hoping to study," she replied and I tuned them out, content to just walk and enjoy the warm air.

A hand slipped into mine and I jumped, glancing down in surprise and back up again to find Kit looking at me expectantly. "What are you doing?" I murmured and he chuckled.

"Playing the part."

It was actually... nice to hold his hand. I'd had hook-ups in the past, but nothing that lasted longer than one night, and I'd never had a real relationship. Just a few casual dates here and there. I'd assumed I wouldn't be one for PDA or hand-holding but with our hands firmly clasped, I found I didn't ever want to let go.

A familiar dark head of hair approached us from the other direction, eyes glued to their phone, and Saylor immediately perked up.

"Xander!"

His cheeks immediately coloured a light pink when he saw her and I rolled my eyes as he scooped a palm over the strands of hair framing his face that were too short for the bun he'd tied his hair back into.

"Oh, hey." He stopped for a second, like he wasn't sure if he was supposed to continue on or join us. "I'm ah, actually heading to the gym and then the library to study. But I'll catch you later?"

Saylor looked slightly disappointed as he walked around us, until he stopped next to her and pressed a quick kiss to her cheek. "See you for dinner at seven."

Kit and Bryn chattered on with my parents as we strode around the park, but I was fairly sure Saylor didn't hear anything they said. Her eyes were glazed and dreamy and had been that way since we'd seen Xander.

"I've got to get back and do some studying actually," Bryn said when Kit suggested stopping for lunch. "But it was lovely meeting you."

I pouted at her and she smirked, the expression so similar to Kit that it took me aback a little. Well, there went my buffer.

We decided to head back to *Cocoa & Rum*, it felt a little less student-y than *The Box* and the food was decent enough just for a quick bite. Thankfully Harley wasn't working, so I didn't have to worry about him blowing our cover... or watching him flirt with Kit again.

My mom beamed around as we sat by one of the larger tables next to the glass window. "Oh, Leo, this is gorgeous! I didn't really take it in last night, we were too excited to see you. Do you come here a lot?"

I shrugged. "Yeah, I guess."

An arm slid around my shoulders and I tensed as Kit leaned in close. "He's being modest. Leo comes and studies here while I work to keep me company."

I leaned forward to grab the menu on the table, despite having the damn thing all but memorized. Kit's arm fell away, just as I'd intended, and I felt like I could breathe a little easier. Yes, we had to sell this if I wanted to keep my mom from meddling in my love life. But I didn't want to wind up with my heart broken and our friendship fractured because I'd let myself lean into him for a bit too long, or forgotten that kissing him wasn't real.

Saylor was sat at the side of the table, with her back to the room, and I decided it would save Kit and I a lot of unnecessary attention if I just diverted it to her instead.

"So what would you even want to study if you came here?"

She shrugged and I tried not to make my relief obvious as my parents focused on my sister. "I don't know, business or something probably."

"Radclyffe is more well known for its focus on the arts," Kit said and I nodded.

"Exactly. You could go anywhere to study business."

She raised one cool, blonde eyebrow at me and I mimicked the movement until we both stared at each other challengingly. "Of course. But Radclyffe has you."

"Ah, sibling love," Kit remarked and my dad chuckled when we both shot him a glare. "Bryn and I are the same sometimes. I didn't want her to leave California to be with me, but it's been nice having her around." He turned to me and I pulled back a little so our faces weren't as close together. "Don't you agree?"

"Yeah," I said vaguely, not even sure what he was really asking me as my eyes fell to his mouth. I swallowed hard and told my eyes to look away, to look at literally anything else. They didn't obey.

Kit's lip ring flicked as he pressed it against his tongue, his mouth tipping up into a smirk as my parents resumed grilling Saylor.

He had a small freckle just under his bottom lip and I didn't think I'd seen it before, but it held all of my attention until all I could think about was tasting it with my tongue.

Warm lips found mine and I jerked back in shock. My mom glanced over curiously, and I let out a shaky laugh. "Just a bug."

I deliberately didn't look Kit's way again, not until his phone started buzzing and he cursed.

"What's wrong?" We hadn't even ordered drinks yet and I felt like we'd been sitting at the table for an age.

"It's Bryn, her place has flooded."

"Shit. Is she okay?"

Kit's fingers flew as he typed out a message but his eyes were calm a moment later when he looked up and found me watching. "She's alright. Her stuff is wrecked though, I'm going to go and see if I can help."

I half-stood with him, catching his hand in mine before abruptly letting go. "Do you want me to come too ?"

He shook his head. "It'll be okay. I'm sorry I can't stay," he said to my parents who waved him off. Before I could process what he was doing, my mouth was captured by his and the breath in my body was being ripped away from me as I fought for composure.

"We're going to talk about this later," he murmured in my ear and I wasn't sure what to say. Talk about Bryn? The kisses he kept laying on me? Something else?

He kissed my cheek, the metal of his lip piercing cold against the flush I could feel in my face. "See you later."

I raised my hand, dazed as he walked away. So much for keeping my distance and protecting my heart.

"Is Bryn okay?"

I'd been nervously pacing for the majority of the afternoon while my parents went out with Saylor to explore. I didn't know what Kit wanted to say to me. Maybe he'd realized what a terrible idea this had been and wanted to call the whole thing off. I hadn't heard a word from him since he'd left *Cocoa &* *Rum* earlier, so there I was, pacing in circles like a mad man until the moment he walked through the door.

"Fine, a little shook up from the shock of it. We're just lucky she was out with us this morning otherwise the ceiling would have come down on her fucking head."

Well if that wasn't a sign from the universe that having a buffer between Kit and me was a good idea, then I didn't know what was.

"I'm glad she's alright. Is she going to stay with us?"

Kit kicked off his shoes and ruffled his hands through his blue hair before flopping down onto his bed. "Actually, no. Jamie offered her the couch at her and Liv's place."

"That was nice of her."

"Yeah."

Silence fell and I twisted my hands together as I watched him stare up at the ceiling.

"Leo."

"Yes?"

"Get over here."

"What?"

He looked at me, the demand clear on his face and I bit my

lip as I moved closer to him. As soon as I was within reach, Kit grabbed my arm, toppling me over half-onto the bed and half-sprawling against his chest. I scrambled to roll away and he sighed.

"That. That right there is what we need to talk about. Why do you keep pulling away from me? How are we supposed to look like a couple when you practically recoil every time I touch you?"

I didn't want to hear these words coming out of his mouth, or see the heat in his eyes. Because what could I tell him? That I pulled away because I liked it too much when he was only being a good friend to me?

"I don't want to take advantage of you," I said quietly, refusing to meet his eyes until his palm cupped my chin and tugged my face back to his.

"Leo, you're not taking anything I'm not freely giving. I'm sorry if me touching you like that makes you feel uncomfortable or—"

"It doesn't," I said quickly, my mouth moving before my brain could think it through.

He paused and I counted his breaths until he spoke. "Then I think there's only one thing for us to do here."

His blue eyes were burning intensely, the color somehow like fire instead of ice and I wanted to drown in the heat.

"What?"

"I'm going to touch you," he said slowly and it felt like my heart stopped. "It doesn't have to mean anything, if you want me to stop I will. But you need to get used to having my hands on you. My mouth. Okay?"

Fuck. What did I do? How would I ever be able to shake free the memory of his lips forming those words as the heat between our bodies seemed to pulse with tension?

"You don't need to prove anything," I said desperately. "I got you into this mess, I can come clean to my parents. So what if she sets me up on a few dates? It's not the worst thing in the world really. Maybe I'll even meet someone and—"

His lips cut off my words and I gasped as his tongue met mine. Now this was a *kiss*. I hadn't even realized he'd been holding back before until his teeth scraped across my bottom lip, sucking it into his mouth, and my dick instantly hardened as heat flooded through my body.

"Kit—" I gasped and he said nothing, just kissed me harder, his mouth devouring mine and I knew I was ruined. I wouldn't be able to look at him ever again and not think of the delicious feeling of his tongue dancing around mine, or the way his breath felt against my skin as we panted together. He wasn't unaffected. No, I could tell that much. I wasn't unattractive, and Kit had a fairly high sex drive based on the frequent hookups he had each week. But he still didn't need to give so much of himself away for me—for something so stupid. But that was Kit in a nutshell, always willing to give his entire soul if it meant helping the people he cared about. I just worried that by the time he was done giving he wouldn't have enough left to sustain himself.

"You're still thinking," he growled and I uncurled the fingers I hadn't even noticed had slid into his hair. "We can fix that."

He took my wrists in one large hand and pinned my arms above my head, smirking down at me as my chest moved rapidly with my breaths.

"Kit," I said desperately. "I don't want this to ruin us. You don't have to do this."

He shook his head. "This isn't going to ruin us, Leo. We can keep things separate, right?"

The air felt heavy as I weighed what he was saying. "Just to sell the ruse?"

I watched him closely and wasn't sure if I imagined the heat in his eyes cooling a couple of degrees when he said, "Of course."

I hesitated and then nodded. It was the only sign he needed. His tee came off over his head and I drank my fill of the sight of him greedily. He'd shaved and his chest was smooth, the muscles in his stomach flexing as he bent over my body to tie the shirt around my hands. Sure, I could probably have broken free easily but that wasn't the point. It was the illusion of being at his mercy, of being the one who surrendered control for once.

Satisfied that I wasn't going to move, Kit dipped back down to straddle my legs as his lips and hands worked to push up my tee, eagerly stroking at my skin like he couldn't get enough of my taste.

I groaned as his tongue flicked across a sensitive spot on my navel and when he looked up at me, his mouth was red from the force of his kisses.

"That's right," he murmured as he licked that same spot again, repeating the motion until my hips jumped up and his tongue wet his bottom lip in anticipation. "Lean into me, Leo. Don't pull away. When I touch you, I want you to beg for it. I want you to need it like you need air to breathe."

God how I wished I Wouldn't have those words in my head forever, but it was a fruitless wish. My mind had sealed this moment away, etched it permanently in the walls of my memory so that I never forgot the way he looked at me, the way he tasted when his mouth sipped from mine. I was losing myself in this, forgetting what the point of it was. It had been too long since I'd been touched like this, and it was *Kit* doing the touching. I was undone, wrecked, and as his hand slid down my zipper the sound raised goosebumps on my skin.

"Kit," I gasped, throat hoarse from the simple pleasure of his touch, his mouth. "Don't take this too far. Don't take this somewhere we can't come back from."

His eyes had darkened to the color of the sea during a storm and when he smiled it was humorless. "If you want me to stop, I will. But we took this too far the moment I had to pretend you were mine."

I didn't know what that was supposed to mean. Lately it felt like he spoke in riddles to me more often than not, but as the air hit my cock and his hair tickled my stomach, the idea of stopping became more than just abhorrent. It was unthinkable. Impossible.

"Yes," I gasped and then his hand was freeing me from my jeans, gripping me so tightly it felt like that was all that anchored me onto this plane when he began to move. My eyes flickered open so I could watch. This was it. The only time I would get with him. I wasn't going to miss a moment.

He shivered as he stroked one hand over my cock, admiring the flush of my skin and the way my head already glistened with moisture. He bent down, keeping his eyes on mine as his tongue swept over my slit, warm and wet and—

"Oh," I expelled a deep breath as he took me in his mouth, the ball on his tongue rolling against my skin and creating an entirely new sensation from anything I'd felt before.

Kit smirked around my cock before driving down and wrapping his lips right the way around me from base to tip. My hips bucked and he hummed in appreciation as I thrust into his mouth.

This was madness. This was *Kit* and even in my filthiest daydreams I never could have imagined it would feel like this with him.

I fucked his mouth, not holding back as he hollowed his cheeks and brushed me with the underside of his tongue.

It was almost embarrassing, the effect he had on me.

"Kit," I said breathlessly, "if you want to stop it has to be now." Before I came so hard I saw stars, spilling onto his tongue. I tried to quiet the thought, not needing it to tip me over the edge, when Kit increased his pace. "Kit," I groaned and he hummed in response, the vibrations of his throat in time with the sweep of his tongue enough to make me cry out as I pumped my hips twice more.

He slowly withdrew his mouth, sucking gently at the tip of my cock before letting it drop from his mouth with a *pop* that had color rushing to my cheeks.

What was I supposed to say to him now? *Thank you?* What we'd just done... What he'd done *to* me, it changed everything. Or, at least, it did for me.

I tugged my hands free from the tee he'd used to tie them back over my head and reached for his zipper, freezing when he caught my wrist in his hand.

Kit looked away, out at his bedroom like he was composing himself before looking back at me. "That's not necessary."

I raised an eyebrow. Not necessary? None of what he'd just done felt *necessary*.

"I'm not the one who was jumping away at *Cocoa & Rum*," he reminded me and I bit my tongue.

"Right." The ruse. Maybe he was attracted to me, I couldn't believe he'd do what he just had otherwise, but clearly attraction was all it was for him.

"Leo—"

My phone buzzed in my back pocket and I reached for it, looking for any reason to escape and distract myself. I re-zipped my jeans and Kit climbed off my lap, his long legs swinging gracefully as I ran a hand through my hair and put my tee back on. The name on the screen was surprising and not entirely welcome, but I would have met with the devil himself if it meant getting out of that room right then. Kit had fucked me thoroughly and despite the fact that I was the one who'd gotten off, he had been the one in control.

"Where are you going?"

Was the worry in his voice because of what we'd just done? Was he already regretting it?

"Out."

"Leo, I—"

"I'll be back soon. Don't wait up." I made sure there was no bite in my voice, just cool indifference. He'd touched me, kissed me, to help me maintain this lie. To make sure that I wouldn't give us away because I was unused to his casual touches or kisses. Nothing more. If he could do this for me and not let it change anything between us, then I could do the same. Even if it broke me in the process. In the end, I wondered if maybe the truth would have been less painful.

CHAPTER FIVE

"I need some legal advice."

I'd sat down in the booth just a couple of minutes ago after ordering a drink at the bar. I'd slung back two shots before deciding to order a tray as well as a rum and coke. To my surprise, Kat had instantly thrown back a shot with the same desperation I'd had.

"Well, to be clear, I'm not a lawyer yet. So if you killed someone I *will* turn you in."

Kat rolled her eyes and I took a moment to appreciate how weird this was. Me and Kat. Alone and buzzed in a bar. *The Box* was relatively busy but combined with the alcohol and my mind trying to replay every moment of Kit going down on me, the buzz of noise was a good distraction.

"I didn't kill anyone. I've... been offered an opportunity."

I narrowed my eyes as she worried her full bottom lip between her teeth. "You realize that sounds shady as hell, right?"

She reached for another shot, shaking her head at me. "God, give me a second to explain instead of jumping down my throat every two seconds Leo."

I clenched my jaw but released my tension with a sigh as she handed me another vodka shot. "Fine, I'll give you what advice I can. But I need something in return." I cleared my throat, looking away awkwardly when she sat forward, green eyes lit up with intrigue.

"What do you want?"

"I want... boy advice."

A giggle exploded out of her and she clapped a hand over her mouth. "Sorry, sorry. Sure. I'll give you boy advice, you give me legal advice. Deal?"

I shook her hand and sat back to survey her. "Tell me."

"You remember Max, right? Jamie's Max?" She looked inclined to babble on so I nodded, waving a hand to tell her to get to the point before she could find a tangent to run. Max had made quite the impression, saving Liv from some drunk idiots and offering Jamie a recording contract to say the least. "Okay, well, in order to open his new studio branch in Sun City, he needs funds right? But he just found out that his parents added a stipulation to his inheritance."

I frowned. It wasn't that uncommon, really I was lucky that the only thing my mother tried to control was my love life and not my *entire* life. "What was the stipulation?"

"In order to access his inheritance, he needs to get married."

I choked on my sip of rum and coke. What was it she'd said? *I've been given an opportunity.* "Kat, what does this have to do with you?" I asked, but I was afraid I already knew the answer.

"Look, I'm not like Liv or Bryn, set up for life with a trust fund. I'm not even like Jamie who's got her independence and the apartment..."

"Right," I prompted and she sighed, fiddling with the buttons on her red top.

"Pretty much all of the money I earn here goes to my

parents. Until I move out, what's mine is theirs. But I can't move out, because I don't have any money. But I don't have any money because—"

"I get the picture," I said, attempting to soften my tone so I wouldn't sound like too much of a dick. "What does this have to do with Max?"

"He needs a wife to access his very big inheritance. We're talking millions, Leo."

"Right...?"

"And I need money so I can finally start living my life *my* way."

"Kat—"

"It was just drunk chit chat at first! But when he found out about this stipulation clause, he made me an offer and Leo—"

"Please tell me you didn't agree to marry him in exchange for money."

"Okay, I won't tell you." She sat back against the booth, watching me stew as I shook my head. "So... Is it illegal?" she said eventually and I blew out a breath. Really, how could I rely on her for boy advice when this was the mess she'd got herself into?

"I don't know," I said truthfully. "Probably? It's definitely unethical. You would probably have to stay married for a while to make it look real."

"We agreed to a year."

I swore, chugging back my drink in response to her words. "So you already signed on for this?"

"I mean, I haven't signed anything yet. He hasn't even given me a ring."

"Look. At best, it's unethical and unfathomably stupid. I mean, you've known him all of five minutes, right? What if he's a serial killer?"

"He's not a—"

I rolled my eyes. "Whatever. At worst, you could both lose everything if someone finds out you cheated the system and your marriage is a fraud."

"So what I'm hearing," Kat said in a tone so much like my sister's that I almost could have laughed if it wasn't so annoying. "Is that as long as nobody finds out, it'll be fine."

"That's not remotely what I said."

Kat sipped happily at a cocktail she'd had sitting there when I'd first joined her. "Good, good. Well, that's my problem sorted. Now you."

I blinked. Had she heard a word I'd said? "Your problem is most definitely not sorted—"

She waved me off. "Enough about me. Tell me about your boy problems, Leo."

I grimaced but leaned in a little closer across the table. "Let's say there's a guy that you're friends with—"

"Kit," she said, taking a casual sip of her drink and ignoring me when I glowered.

"—and sometimes he says stuff to you that kind of makes it seem like he might... feel things for you."

"What kind of stuff?" Kat's eyes gleamed and I swallowed hard against my suddenly dry mouth.

"Um, something about being a masterpiece? And a weird conversation with another guy about whose drink I wanted? Hypothetically, of course," I added hastily.

"Of course," Kat repeated dryly.

"Plus, hypothetically, let's say he was happy to do me a favor and pretend to be my boyfriend while my parents visited. And maybe as part of that scheme, we made out? Heavily?"

At some point, Kat's mouth had dropped open and when she reached across the table to touch my hand I was too startled to move away. "Oh, sweetie."

What was that supposed to mean?

"Fake boyfriend, fake fiancee... we have more in common than you would have thought, huh?"

I opened my mouth and then closed it again. "What does it mean? You're supposed to be giving me advice!"

"My advice," she said around a big gulp of her drink, "is to ride it out." Kat threw an exaggerated wink at me and I wrinkled my nose.

"You're obnoxious when you're drunk," I said stiffly and she sniffed, falling back against her seat with a thump.

"You're an obnoxious."

"That doesn't even make sense." I rubbed my eyes and reached for one of the last shots on the tray.

She sighed heavily and looked at me with an odd sheen to her eyes. "You and Kit are the will-they-won't-they people of the group. Just go with it, find out if you're a will or a won't."

Just go with it. That was what I'd told Kit when my parents had just arrived. It was what he'd said to taunt me after we'd schemed up our ruse. Maybe I needed to take my own advice.

"You make a weird amount of sense for someone who's going to fake-marry a serial killer."

"Hey," she said sharply and I looked up in surprise before relaxing when she giggled. "That's my fake-fiance you're talking about."

I laughed and when she joined in I felt a strange sense of ease I hadn't been expecting to find when I'd come to meet her. "Just go with it," I murmured and she nodded like I'd asked a question.

"Just go with it."

We sipped our drinks in silence for a moment before both our phones went off at the same time.

"Group chat," I murmured absently and Kat nodded, scrolling through the messages. I would have done the same if I hadn't been distracted by the familiar figures of my sister and

Xander strolling in. He'd decided to take her to dinner *here?* Well, I guess it was casual, but still. I ducked slightly when Saylor turned toward our booth and Kat raised her eyes from her phone long enough to watch me in bemusement.

"What are you doing?"

"Hiding from my sister."

She nodded, her brows furrowing as she continued, "Right. Why, exactly?"

"Because she's on a date with Xander and I want to spy on them."

Kat snorted and I sat up slowly, feeling a little embarrassed after saying that aloud. "Sounds like a healthy relationship."

"I didn't know she was going to be here," I pointed out and Kat just hummed in response. "What did they say in the chat, anyway?"

"They're coming here."

They? "Who?"

"Everyone."

Fuck. I bit my lip. I'd relaxed a little since I'd arrived, but I wasn't sure I was ready to face Kit yet. Especially not while surrounded by our friends.

"We can leave if you want," Kat said softly and it was a genuinely sweet offer, her green eyes big and round in her face as she watched me.

"No," I said eventually, "thank you. I'll have to see him at some point, it might as well be now."

"Then I think we're going to need more drinks," Kat said, slapping her palm down on to the table before heading up to the bar and leaving me with a perfect view of Saylor and Xander a couple of booths down.

Jamie was the first of the group to arrive and I smiled tightly at her as she slid into the booth opposite me. It wasn't that I had a problem with her, exactly, it was just that where

Jamie went, trouble often followed and it was exhausting sometimes.

"You're early," I commented and she brushed her chin-length dark hair out of her face as she smirked.

"You sound surprised. I do only live around the corner."

True. But that didn't stop her from being late the majority of the time we met as a group at *The Box*. She looked at home in the booth, the hot pink lighting making her look even grungier than usual in her cropped white top and deep purple lipstick.

God, this was awkward. I'd never really had to speak with her one-on-one like this and I had no idea what to say.

"So..." I began and then let out an audible breath of relief when I spotted Kit and Ryan heading our way. "Oh, thank god," I muttered and Jamie's dark eyes glittered with amusement.

My initial relief didn't last though, not when my gaze locked with Kit's and stayed there, like he commanded gravity, sucking all the air out of the room. I blinked first, reaching absently for the shot Kat was passing me on her way back from the bar and slugging it back quickly.

"Is that Xander?" Ryan said, oblivious to what was going on between me and Kit. "We should ask if he wants to join us."

Before I could offer a single word of disagreement, Ryan was striding over to Saylor and Xander and then doing a double-take when he looked at her and probably noticed her resemblance to me.

Kit sat down next to me and it felt like I was a live wire, my body hyper aware of the scant space between our bodies, my hair raising on my arms. I shuffled away slightly, trying to give myself some space to breathe air that didn't smell of him, but he moved with me.

I frowned before looking up to see why—Xander and Saylor were scooting onto the bench next to us.

"You don't have to sit here," I said to them both and Xander raised an eyebrow. "You can go back to your date." I threw a look in Ryan's direction and he winced.

"Ah sorry. I just—you have to be Leo's sister, right? I mean, you're practically identical."

Saylor grinned and held out her hand for Ry to shake. "Saylor. And yes, we get that a lot which I've always found weird considering I'm clearly a lot prettier than Lee-Lee."

To anyone else, Saylor's words might have seemed flirtatious. But I knew that she was simply being her usual, confident self.

Kat caught my eye and mouthed *Lee-Lee* excitedly and I gave her a deadpan look in return.

"Where's Liv?" I asked casually, attempting to divert the conversation, and Jamie frowned, the expression looking too serious on her usually care-free face.

"At home in her room last I checked. She didn't want to come out. I think Bryn's with her."

"Thanks again for letting her stay with you," Kit said smoothly and even the sound of his voice had my body tensing as I fought to keep myself in the present, rather than remembering the way that same voice had sounded when he'd told me he wanted me to beg for him. The conversation flowed around me and I didn't take any of it in, too busy trying to ignore the warmth of Kit's body, the occasional brush of his hand.

I snapped to attention when Saylor reached for one of the shots Kat had brought to the table earlier, leaning across Kit to snag her wrist. "What are you doing?"

One blonde eyebrow rose. "Drinking. Or, I would be if I wasn't currently having a conversation with you."

I glowered. "You're not twenty-one."

"So?"

"*So*," I repeated, "it's illegal, and I don't really want to have to explain to Mom and Dad how their kid daughter got trashed with my friends."

Saylor rolled her eyes and I could feel the stares of everyone at the table as they watched this battle of wills. "Kid daughter? You realize I'm like, two years younger than you. That means I'm old enough to have a baby, join the army, buy a gun, but *alcohol* is where this great country draws the line?" She scoffed and I released her hand, frowning when she tossed back the shot effortlessly. "Is it really any wonder he wants to be a lawyer? You've got the biggest hard-on for the rules, it's insane."

"Please don't ever say *hard-on* to me again," I mumbled as I sat back in my seat and jumped when Kit's arm curled around my waist beneath the table.

"You two are cute," Jamie said, her full mouth curving in a way that suggested she was only partially joking. "Makes me wish I had a sibling."

"Take mine," Saylor and I said at the same time and then glared at each other. I wasn't sure if it was my bickering with my sister, or the comfort of Kit's arm around me, but for a second, it felt like everything was going to be just fine.

CHAPTER SIX

"You know, there's more to life than studying." Saylor scrolled on her phone opposite me at the breakfast bar as I recapped my highlighter pen.

"Thanks for the advice," I said dryly and sighed when she didn't look up. "I'm sorry."

That got her attention. "For what?"

I looked away, clearing my throat awkwardly. "Not calling. Or texting. Or visiting."

"Well when you list it all out like that..." She laughed. "I get it. Communication is not your strong suit and I know you get caught up working. Plus, the phone goes both ways."

I frowned. That was true. "Why haven't *you* called or texted *me*?"

Another laugh from her made my frown deepen. "Because *life*, Leo." We stared at each other for a moment before she sighed. "We both suck. We'll both do better. Agreed?"

I held out my hand and she shook it firmly. "Agreed."

"Nice doing business with you."

She was a dork in the best way and I hadn't realized how

much I'd missed her until she was here with me. We'd been fairly close when we'd been growing up and had even leaned into the whole 'you guys could be twins' thing. I slapped her hand away from my glass of orange juice. She may be my sister, but that didn't mean I wanted her mouth on my cup.

"Gross. Get your own."

"Some things don't change," she said fondly as she stood and walked to the cupboard to grab a glass with enough confidence and familiarity it was almost like she'd always been there. "So tell me about you and Kit."

"What do you want to know?" I said carefully and dropped my eyes back to the textbook I'd been highlighting.

"How did you get together?"

I swallowed, considering my answer carefully. The best lies were the ones rooted in truth, after all. "We were friends and then I kissed him." Not technically untrue.

"Just out of the blue?" Saylor leaned forward, dark eyes alight with intrigue, close enough that I could see the very light dusting of freckles on her nose.

"Pretty much," I admitted. "You know communication isn't my strong suit," I joked, repeating her own words back to her, my voice sounding only slightly strangled.

"How long have you liked him for?" She wrapped both hands around her glass of juice like we were moms gossiping on a front porch in the autumn and I nearly laughed at her sudden resemblance to our mother.

"Honestly?" I took a deep breath and shrugged. "I can't really remember a time when I didn't like him."

"I like seeing you happy," she said, smiling and I smiled back. I'd never been more stressed or confused in my life, but I supposed it was true that I was happy too. Even if this thing with Kit was just temporary, it had still been a gift of sorts. It was how I'd be feeling when it ended that concerned me.

"Did I hear my name?" Kit said casually as he strolled into the kitchen. There was a smear of paint on his face and his white tee clung to his chest in a way that I found irritatingly distracting. It, too, was covered in paint. We were almost complete opposites, but seeing him rumpled and messy, happy and paint-splattered, my heart swelled.

"Leo was just telling me how he's liked you forever," Saylor said before I could do more than glance at her in alarm.

"Was he now?" Kit's smile grew, his tongue piercing flashing in the light when he chuckled. "Tell me more, Leo."

I straightened in my chair and shrugged casually. "And inflate your ego further? I don't think so."

"When he kissed you, were you shocked? Or did you suspect he liked you?"

"Suspect? No." Kit leaned against the counter by the sink and I swiveled in my chair so I could keep him in my eyesight. "Hope? Of course. Nobody likes an unrequited crush. Besides," he said, eyes heavy on mine as a spark of something seemed to jump between us, "it feels like I've liked Leo forever too."

Warmth swept through me and I wished desperately that I could erase the memory of those words. This was just cruel. Definitely more painful than having to endure the surprise dates my mom would set me up on.

I unclenched my jaw and looked at Kit before shaking my head. "Saylor I—"

I hadn't even realized Kit was moving until his warm hand cupped my chin and tilted my face upwards, his mouth covering mine and trapping the confession I'd been about to spill. He knew me too well. He licked into my mouth and a groan rumbled through his chest, so deep it nearly seemed real. Maybe Kit should ditch art and become an actor, because the way he was kissing me? Well, if I hadn't already been in love with him, I definitely would have been by now.

"How can anyone not like him?" Kit said when he broke the kiss, his mouth close to mine as his blue eyes burned into me.

"Okay well, this just got awkward so I'm going now."

I didn't acknowledge Saylor's words and neither did Kit, his gaze kept solely on me.

"Why?" he said and I knew what he was asking—why had I nearly told my sister everything?

"Because this is getting messier by the day and I just don't know if it's a good idea any more."

Kit nodded slowly, dropping his hand from my face and taking a step back. "Well, your parents will be gone in a few days right? And then you won't have to endure any more of this," he said, gesturing to the space between us and my still-tingling lips before he moved past me and the front door slammed shut.

I didn't even try to stop him. How could I tell him that I wanted to come clean not because I didn't like it when he touched me... but because I liked it too much?

I felt kind of bad going to class while my parents were visiting, but it was one of the ones I absolutely couldn't miss. Mostly because it was one of the only classes I had any exams left to complete.

So I'd gotten up that morning as quietly as possible so I didn't wake up Kit and had left for class early to study in the library beforehand.

Bryn met me on my way into the lecture hall and smiled tiredly.

"Long night on the couch?"

"Sort of. But I don't mind, it was nice of them to let me stay after my place flooded."

"Well, if you get bored of their couch you can always try out ours."

Bryn laughed. "I appreciate it." We found seats near the back of the room and the chatter around us echoed slightly thanks to the high ceilings. "So, should I even ask about what's going on with you and my brother?"

"Um, he's just doing me a favor while my parents are here."

"Doing you a favor, huh. Is that what they're calling it these days?" Bryn teased, her eyes sparkling in the same shade of blue that Kit's did when he was amused.

Thankfully, she dropped the subject, not saying anything more about it as class began, and I found myself relieved. I didn't want to spend every waking moment thinking about Kit, about how he'd touched me and kissed me like it meant something. Exam prep was actually a welcome distraction.

My notes were detailed and I was actually feeling good about the essay plan I'd drafted and turned in before, so I was surprised when the professor asked me to stay behind. Honestly, I hadn't even realized she'd known my name. Some of our classes were large, it would have been difficult for her to keep up with every one of her students.

"Ah, Leo. Excellent. I was hoping you might be able to help me with something?"

"Of course," I said, surprised, and she gestured behind me, beckoning someone over. I blinked, recognizing the gold-tanned skin and crooked grin heading my way. "Harley. I didn't realize—"

"That we were on the same course? Yeah I figured." He

dimpled at me, as if to reduce any bite the words might have held.

"Oh! You two already know each other. Well, that will make this easier."

I raised an eyebrow. "He works with my... friend. What exactly do you need us for?"

"Based on the work you've submitted thus far, I think you'll be very comfortable in the upcoming examination for this unit."

I smiled. "Thank you, ma'am."

"Harley, could use a little guidance, however. I felt that you may be a good fit as a study buddy of sorts."

"Oh," I said brilliantly and then cleared my throat. "I mean, of course. No problem." I looked at Harley and tried my best approximation of a friendly expression. "I'd be happy to help."

"I appreciate it," he said, warmth cradling every word and I flushed a little. "Walk you out?"

I nodded and said a goodbye to Professor Frey as we made our way outside. Bryn had gone on without me, and I didn't mind. She was still settling in at Jamie's and had looked a little dead on her feet. Not that I'd slept brilliantly last night either. I'd met with Kat again at *The Box* and let her ply me with drinks at the bar while she worked. Kit had either been asleep or pretending by the time I'd stumbled in, drunk as fuck but surprisingly buoyant after seeing Kat. I'd never been good at making friends, but Kat made it feel easy.

"Earth to Leo," Harley said, a light chuckle following the words. "Listen, if you only said yes because Frey asked—"

"I didn't," I said quickly, smiling through the lie. "I'm happy to help you. Plus it gives me a chance to test my own knowledge."

"Well, that does make me feel better."

A laugh slipped out of me and faded quickly as I spotted

Kit up ahead with Saylor, sitting on a bench under the shade of a leafy-green tree. Clearly they'd come to meet me after class and, judging by the muscle ticking in Kit's jaw, weren't thrilled about having to wait so long.

"Sorry guys, I didn't know you would be here waiting for me or I'd have hurried. The professor kept us back."

"Bryn went past about ten minutes ago," Kit said, his tone weirdly even and I peered at him in confusion. *Why did he seem... mad?*

"Yeah," I said slowly, "she just kept *us* back. She wanted to see if I'd help Harley study for our final."

I hadn't even realized that the air had felt tense until it dissipated. Kit took half a step closer to me on the opposite side to Harley, his hand brushing mine.

"That's nice of you."

"It really is," Harley said, a kind of mischief in his eyes that was going straight over my head as he stared at Kit. "I don't know how I'll repay him."

"It's not a big deal," I said, glancing between the two of them and shooting a look of pure bewilderment at my sister as she fought a grin.

"Well, I have a shift to get to," Harley said as he took a step back from us and handed me a slip of paper I hadn't even noticed him holding. "Text me when you want to see me. I'll be waiting."

I nodded and slipped it into my pocket as he walked away. "He was friendly," I remarked as Saylor laughed.

"Don't ever change, Lee-Lee."

I pushed her away as she attempted to ruffle my hair. "Don't call me that."

Kit had been quiet for too long and it was starting to unnerve me. Was this about yesterday? "What's wrong with you?" I said, a little more bluntly than I'd intended. "I mean, are you okay?"

"Of course, why wouldn't I be?"

My sister snorted at Kit's response and I clenched my jaw until my teeth creaked. Sometimes it was frustrating feeling like everyone else was in on some joke that I didn't get. I wasn't unintelligent, some things just passed me by no matter how hard I tried to understand them or learn the cues.

"Whatever," I muttered, walking on and trying to enjoy the breeze rustling the trees as it offered a respite from the oppressive heat that seemed to have kicked up a notch the past few days.

"Hey," Kit caught my hand and Saylor continued walking, giving us a moment of privacy. "I'm sorry. I just didn't like how... friendly he was being with you."

I blinked. "You think he was interested in me? As in, hitting on me?" I snorted but let the smile fade away as Kit nodded. "For the record, I think that's ridiculous. But I get why you acted so weird."

"You do?"

"Of course, Saylor was standing right there. If Harley was flirting with me then it would be strange for my boyfriend not to be a little jealous, right?"

"Right," he said after a moment's hesitation. "Let's just get back home. Your mom said something about going bowling?"

I groaned and the sound sent a little heat flaring in Kit's eyes. "Ugh. I didn't even know we *had* bowling around here. She's like a bloodhound, sniffing out any lane within a hundred feet."

Saylor laughed as we caught up to her. "You heard about bowling then? Leo's just upset because Mom always wins."

"You're a sore loser?" Kit grinned and the sight knocked the breath out of me for a moment. "How did I not know that about you?"

"Because I never lose," I said coolly and Kit leaned in close, a smirk playing on his lips.

"I'll remember you said that." There was an unmistakable note of *want* in his voice that made me shiver as my mind whirled, thinking about all the different ways we could compete.

"I'll remind you whenever necessary," I said with more confidence than I felt and when he licked his lips in response I fought to keep my expression blank even as my dick twitched.

"Let's go bowling," Kit said with a raised eyebrow and Saylor looked between us with a knowing look on her face, softening her eyes.

"Let's," I said, hoping I wasn't going to regret taunting him.

"Better luck next time, sweetie," my mom crowed as I walked back to retrieve another ball. I might have been a sore loser, but *she* was a sore winner.

I grabbed another ball for the second half of my turn and furrowed my brow when Kit stood up and walked towards me.

"Come on," he said, scuffing his converse against the cheap laminate flooring as he led me over to the lane.

"What are you doing?"

"Helping."

"Aw, Lee-Lee sucks so much he has to have his boyfriend show him how to do it," Saylor called and I glared at her as she sucked down what could only be described as a bucket full of soda. While I enjoyed spending time with my family, especially considering I hadn't seen them for a while, I wished we could have been anywhere but this bowling alley. Everything was sticky, even the floor, and the smell of burgers was making me feel queasy after an hour without any break.

Kit placed his hands on my waist, the warmth from his hands soaking into me before he let them drop. His breath tickled my ear as he leaned in to speak. "Focus on me."

"What?" Did he really think that focusing on him was going to make me less distracted? If anything I was going to suck more with him standing so close, the scent of vanilla and sandalwood aftershave washing over me, fogging my senses.

"The lights, the noise, they're grating on you right now aren't they?"

I hadn't really realized it until he'd said it, but it was true. The whole room felt *loud*, everything from the flashing lights above the lane that glittered a strange purple to the flatscreens above the benches that called out the scores and played silly little animations that shrilled and thundered just as much as the actual balls knocking down the pins. It made it hard to think, like this room operated on a frequency that scrambled my brain.

"Why does it constantly smell like burgers?" I complained and he chuckled.

"It's just math," Kit said quietly. "Angles and speed. You're good at math right? So just focus on me, let all the sound zero down and then throw the ball." He stood at my side, his words soft and the openness on his face encouraging. I met his eyes and found only comfort, understanding.

I let out a slow breath and did as he said, doing my best to ignore the lights and sounds that seemed overly vivid and focused only on the sound of Kit's breathing next to me as I threw the ball.

"Spare!" The corny game show host's voice on the flatscreens announced and I grinned as I turned to look at Kit and found him watching me, a small smile on his lips. I wanted to kiss him, I realized. More badly than I ever had before. I wasn't stupid, I knew I was probably on the spectrum or ADD or something, but Kit had never judged me or made me feel less-than. He saw me, possibly better than I saw myself.

My mom squealed as she bounded up for her turn and planted a kiss on first my cheek and then Kit's. "Well done, sweetie! A spare! Next time will be a strike, I know it."

I smiled slightly, enjoying seeing her happy. I took her spot on the bench next to my dad in the booth and Kit plopped down next to my sister. They teased each other just like Bryn did whenever she was around Kit, and that was one of the hardest things to know. Kit fit in here, he felt like family, like he was meant to be by my side. If the universe had a plan for me, I had no doubts that he was in it. It wasn't the universe's fault that I'd got greedy and wanted more.

"He's good for you," my dad murmured quietly and I looked up in surprise to find him watching me steadily. "I like how you are with him. You've picked a good one there, son."

"Thanks, Dad," I said quietly, trying not to think about the fact that I hadn't picked anything. I'd stolen Kit, and sooner than I would ever be able to bear I would have to give him up. To pretend like there was never anything more between us than friendship. I wasn't sure if it would kill me more that I'd got to experience this with him, to know that this kind of love, and ease, was out there and I'd never have more of it than this. Or whether never having got this time with him would have been worse. The wondering, the yearning... I was greedy. I wasn't sure I would ever have enough of him.

"Did you guys decide how long you're staying for?" I asked quietly, dreading the answer as he nodded.

"I think we'll take off in a couple days. You know your mom doesn't like to leave the kids for too long."

I did know. My mom worked as a teacher and it was her passion, the same way being a lawyer was mine. My dad had retired after a car accident had made it impossible for him to operate any more.

"Are you keeping yourself busy?"

To my surprise, he smiled. "I'm teaching classes a couple times a week in Tucson."

I blinked. "That's amazing."

"I never thought I'd find anything as fulfilling as surgery, but it turns out I've got the teaching bug just like your mother." I laughed with him and reached for my own soda. "I think your sister may stay for a few days extra. I think she likes it here."

He wasn't wrong, and it was more than just me or her date with Xander. Something about being in Sun City had made her light up in a way I hadn't even noticed had been missing until I saw it again. That probably made me a bad brother, but at least I saw it now.

"I'll look out for her."

"I know," he said, his smile crinkling the corners of his eyes as we watched her. "Looks like I'm up!"

Kit looked at me, a laugh still on his mouth as he listened to whatever my sister was telling him, and the warmth in my chest refused to dissipate.

"Maybe you'll win after all," my mom said breathlessly as she sat down and I nodded without paying too much attention to what she meant, keeping my eyes on Kit.

"Yeah, maybe," I said vaguely as a heat burned in his eyes that had my body feeling like it was a live wire. A kernel of determination flared and I broke our eye contact so I could think a little more clearly. Who said I had to let him go? Maybe if I played my part well enough, we wouldn't be playing a part at all.

I looked out at the lanes as my dad threw his ball and

swallowed past the lump in my throat. Was I really going to do this? To fight for him even though I knew I would probably end up with my heart broken even worse than it would be if we'd just gone back to being friends when my family left? My eyes found Kit as one of his hands ruffled his hair. *Yeah. Yes.* I was going to try and win the heart of my best friend.

I pulled out my phone and shot a quick text off to Kat before I could change my mind.

Leo: Hypothetically, how would I make my fake boyfriend real?

CHAPTER SEVEN

I WAS STILL DEBATING THE BEST WAY TO TEST THE water with Kit a full day later and was no closer to having a concrete plan. Of course, that frustrated Kat more than anything. She was friends with Jamie, possibly the most impulsive person I'd ever met, and was used to her slightly more brutal methods. That wasn't my style. I didn't want to ruin things between me and Kit. I wanted to see if he only wanted to be friends, or if he was open to the possibility of something more. We'd kissed, fuck—we'd more than kissed, and maybe I was stupid or naive but I didn't want to believe it meant nothing.

"Maybe you should ask him for me."

"You're not in third grade, Leo. If you're worried about asking him, then get him drunk first. Be an adult about it." Kat licked the line of sugar from the rim of her glass and then winced as she sipped her cocktail.

"Is alcohol the solution you give to everyone's problems? Or just mine?" I said dryly as I accepted the nachos she slid my way.

"I'm just saying, sometimes people say things when they're wasted that they wouldn't when they're sober."

"Are you speaking from experience?"

She adjusted one of the thin straps of her black top and avoided my eyes as she scoffed. "What? No. Of course not."

I waited her out, munching on nachos and drinking my beer as she fidgeted. If there was one thing Kat struggled with, it was silence.

"Okay, yes, Max may have said some things to me the other night."

"Like?"

Half of her cocktail disappeared in the massive gulp she took. "None of your business."

"Seriously? So you can ask me to describe my sexual encounter with Kit but me asking about a conversation between you and Max is too much?"

"Well, you didn't actually give me those details."

I rolled my eyes at the hopeful look on her face. "Do you have any advice outside of alcohol and sex?"

She paused, pouting her mouth as she considered my words. "No, not really." I snorted and she laughed with me. "If you don't want to seduce him or get him drunk, and you don't want to just ask him outright because you're a chicken, then you only have one other option."

"Oh?"

Her smile made me uneasy, it felt like the embodiment of chaos and mischief, especially when she blinked at me innocently. "You need to make him so feral with jealousy that if he does feel something for you, he'll lose control to claim you as his."

I wrinkled my nose, tapping my fingers absently on the side of my glass to the indie pop song *The Box* was playing. *Claim me as his?* She made it sound so... caveman. "I don't want to hurt or manipulate him."

"You're not," she needled, wiping away the smudge of her pink lipstick on her glass. "You're just making it clear that you have options, that you're not just going to wait around for him to step up and declare his intentions."

"Have you been reading regency romance again?"

Kat sniffed before trying, and failing, to hold back a grin. "Maybe." I opened my mouth but she shook her head. "Just think about it, okay? The worst that could happen is he doesn't get jealous and you know where you stand, friendship intact."

"I guess," I said quietly. "Anyway, I have to get back to the house, my parents are leaving tomorrow so I said I'd have dinner with them tonight."

"Sure thing." She stood and stretched and I glowered at the guy in the booth behind us, checking out her ass over the head of his girlfriend. "You'll text me?"

I nodded as I walked her out of the bar. We'd been chatting a lot recently, normally over text, and I was surprised at how much I enjoyed her company. Somehow, I'd stumbled into another friendship that felt just as comfortable as the one between me and Kit. "Thank you. For the advice," I added when she looked up curiously.

"Say hi to Kit for me," she called as she strode off towards the direction of campus. I wasn't quite sure where her parents lived but maybe she wasn't heading there.

"Do you want me to walk you back?" It was getting dark and the parks weren't hugely safe once the sun went down.

Kat shook her head and blew me a kiss, walking backwards before spinning around. I'd text her later to make sure she got home safe anyway.

I walked in the opposite direction to her, enjoying the smell of the grass and warm earth as nature settled in for the night and the city lights began to glow a little brighter as the dark crept in. The walk was short, but it helped clear my head a little after the drinks I'd shared with Kat.

The house was lit up by the time I reached it, the kitchen lights illuminating the sides of the house through the windows and I sniffed cautiously as I entered, hoping that Xander hadn't been cooking. But nothing smelled burned, which was a good sign, and when I walked into the lounge I paused at the sight of Kit and Xander sitting with my family and passing around pizza boxes.

"I thought we were going out for dinner?"

"Leo!" My mom smiled as she turned. "You're just in time, sweetheart. We thought it might be nice to have a more relaxed night in, maybe play some games."

"Game night?" I couldn't hide my hope and Saylor grinned at me from Xander's side on the couch.

Game night had always been my favorite family night, especially when we played—

"Scrabble?" Kit said, coming out from behind me where he'd gone to retrieve plates and napkins judging by the stack in his arms, and nodded to the table where the box was already out. I took some plates out of his hands and tried to swallow. *Scrabble* shouldn't have sounded like a dirty word, it shouldn't have turned me on, but Kit whispering it in my ear when he *knew* how much I loved that game...

Yeah. It did things to me.

"Here, I saved you a box. I know you don't like to share."

I stared at him as I put the plates on the coffee table in front of the sofa and took the box he was offering me. He was right. Communal foods that everyone had their hands in was not my thing.

I cleared my throat. "Thank you." We dug in and I chewed quietly as they chatted amongst themselves. Maybe it was the alcohol in my system, or maybe Kat had been right. Doing nothing hadn't exactly worked for me thus far, so if I wanted Kit to be mine—really mine—then I needed to do something to make it happen.

By the time the plates were cleared away and the Scrabble board was brought out, I'd talked myself in and out of various plans a dozen times. I was probably going to have to sleep on it. Of course, that was easier said than done when the person I was so torn up about would be sleeping right next to me.

After three rounds of Scrabble that I won, and one round of Boggle that I didn't, we all headed up to bed so my parents could get on the road early the next day. Nerves curled inside my stomach like butterflies flapping their wings and I felt vaguely sick as Kit closed his bedroom door behind us. There was no reason for me to feel so nervous tonight versus any of the other nights I'd spent in his bed, listening to the soothing sound of his breathing, surrounded by his smell. Maybe it was because of the realization I'd had, the decision I'd made, that made this night feel different. More electric. Or maybe it was the way he watched me as he undressed, hungry but knowing, until he climbed under the covers in nothing but his boxers.

"Has it been nice having them here?" he said quietly once I was settled next to him. I nodded and then realized he couldn't see me in the dark.

"Yeah, I hadn't realized how much I'd been missing them." I moved my feet against the covers absently, enjoying the sensation of the duvet on my toes. It was an odd habit, but it relaxed me and thankfully Kit didn't seem to mind the slight motion of my legs under the sheets. "Do you miss your parents?"

"Sometimes," he mused. "But I have Bryn and that helps. I think my mom is actually coming down here soon."

"Cool," I said, unsure what else to say, and knew he was smiling at me from the sound of his voice when he next spoke.

"I think she'd like you."

"Your mom?"

"Yeah."

"My parents love you," I said without thinking and then winced into the dark. "They think you're perfect for me."

"I am."

My heartbeat quickened and I licked my lips before daring to reply. "Oh?"

"I played the perfect boyfriend, Leo. Did you expect anything less?"

Right. Playing. My jaw clenched and I had to force the words out past my teeth and the unexpected surge of anger. "And when you had me in this bed? You were just playing then too?"

"Weren't you?" Kit said, voice hushed, and I felt like I was burning with the desire to tell him not to be ridiculous. That I wanted him, no pretending required. It felt like a test, like a precipice that if I jumped off of I'd never land correctly.

"Of course," I said, cursing my own cowardice even as my body leaned in closer to him.

"Right."

I sighed and rolled away from him so I faced the room. The house was silent, just the city sounds outside trickling in through the window we'd cracked to help with the heat and Kit's breathing, in sync with my own.

"Where were you tonight? Before you got home?"

Was this what Kat had been talking about? Was this jealousy? How was I supposed to play this? "Why does it matter?"

He fell silent before finally saying, "I guess it doesn't."

I let him stew for a few minutes longer before confessing, "I was out with Kat."

"Kat?" He scoffed and I understood his disbelief. "So you two are friends now?"

"We've been talking recently."

"About what?"

"Stuff."

I bit my lip. What did this mean? Was Kit jealous because he was worried I'd been seeing someone romantically? Or was he just mad to be left out of the loop as one of my friends? My closest friend, really.

"We should get some sleep," I said finally. "I have my first session tutoring Harley tomorrow and I want to see my parents off before they leave too."

"You're seeing Harley?"

I furrowed my brow, rolling over to search what little I could see of Kit's face in the dark. "Yes. I mean, it's only tutoring so I doubt my parents would find it suspicious anyway but they'll be gone by the time I leave. Why? Is it an issue?"

"Nope," Kit bit out and I blinked, surprised by the coldness of his voice. "No problem at all."

"Okay," I said slowly. "Good, because tomorrow everything can go back to the way it was before my parents got here."

"Right. Fine."

"Fine," I repeated and he made a quiet sound that might have been a growl.

"Go to sleep, Leo."

I rolled back over and in the dark, I smiled.

CHAPTER EIGHT

"I'M SORRY SWEETHEART, I KNOW YOU WERE probably looking forward to having your bed back. Though," my mom added with a wink, "I'm sure it's no hardship sharing with this handsome young man." She slung an arm around Kit's waist and he laughed.

"They seem to think they can fix whatever the issue with the car is by tomorrow afternoon. So I guess you've got us for another day," my dad said as he hung up the phone and sat down on the couch next to me. "It's so strange though, we had it serviced right before we drove down and it was fine." He shook his head.

"You're always welcome," I said honestly and then groaned. "But I'm going out in a little while to tutor someone in my class, so you'll have to entertain yourselves for a bit."

"Don't you worry about that," my mom fussed as she dug around in her purse for something. "We were thinking of going over to that diner near the mall for a late breakfast anyway. Are you guys around this evening or did you have plans already?" She looked between me and Kit and I met his eyes briefly before looking away. He'd probably thought he was in the clear today, was likely planning a wild night of partying and drunken hook-ups just because he could—

"No plans," Kit said, smiling and raising an eyebrow at me ever so slightly, like a challenge. "We should go out for food tonight."

"Well, I'm taking the car breaking down as a sign that I'm supposed to stick around here for a bit longer." Saylor glanced in the direction of the hall, as if she could see all the way to Xander's room through the walls. "But I'm going out with Xander tonight, so we can't join you guys."

"Does Xander know that?" I said dryly and she grinned, which didn't reassure me in the least.

"Dinner sounds like a great idea, Kit," my mom gushed and I wasn't sure I could agree. A small, cozy dinner with just me, Kit, and my parents? Why had he suggested this?

"Okay, well, I have to go and meet Harley for our tutoring session." I hesitated when I stood up and paused to kiss my mom on the cheek, inhaling her familiar lilac perfume. "I'm happy I get to be with you guys for another night."

"I'll go with you guys to sort out the car," Kit volunteered, surprising me. His eyes were a little too wide, his smile a shade too bright, he almost looked guilty and that really baffled me.

I glanced at my phone, mostly to give myself a second to compose myself, and cursed when I saw the time. "I have to go and meet Harley, sorry. I'll see you when I get back."

Kit's face darkened at the second mention of Harley's name and I watched in fascination for a second before shaking myself. If he was just pretending, then why did it look like he actually cared? Maybe he did care but, like me, was choosing not to implode our relationship with feelings other than platonic ones. Maybe he didn't think we were worth it, maybe for him it was just a crush. I was worried it had spiraled into a lot more than that for me.

I stepped close to him, trying not to suck down the scent of his aftershave greedily as I moved into his space and pressed my lips to his cheek, the slight morning stubble there scratching against my face in a way that made me feel awkwardly turned on considering my parents were just paces away from us.

"I'll see you later."

"Bye," he murmured, eyes hooded as I stepped away. Suddenly his arm flew out and caught my hand before I could get too far and his lips met mine in a fleeting crash of hunger that I knew I would be feeling on my skin for the rest of the day. He smirked as he let go and I tried to remember how to breathe. Could someone really be that good at pretending?

"Your essay looks good," I said, leaning in close to Harley as I pointed out a few paragraphs in particular, careful not to knock his coffee over. "But these could use tightening up a little. You're not citing enough precedents here to support the foundation of your argument."

Our upcoming exam was largely essay based. Some of it was application based, defending or creating arguments, but the majority of it was connected to case studies and how specific cases had helped effect or shape the law. I'd never had any trouble remembering names or dates, but it didn't come easily to everyone. Harley included.

"Right, got it. Thank you. Honestly, you're a lifesaver, Leo."

I looked up and found I was sitting a lot closer to him than I'd realized—close enough to see that the flecks in his eyes were almost gold and that his lashes were blonde at the tips.

I cleared my throat, leaning back and nodding as I avoided his eyes by looking around at the tables nearby. "Of course. I'm happy to help."

"I'm lucky it was you that Frey asked to help me. I've seen you in class, scribbling your notes almost as fast as the professor can speak."

I quirked my mouth. "And here I didn't even realize we shared a class." I took a sip of the latte I'd ordered and paused after I swallowed. "If you knew who I was, then why did you ask Kit about me the other night?"

Harley dimpled at me, his smile big and a little embarrassed even as it failed to warm his eyes. "I was hoping he'd introduce me."

"To me?" I asked, raising my eyebrows as I watched a girl with bright pink hair pack away her laptop. "Why?

"Is it so unbelievable that I'd want to get to know you?" He laughed and anyone else might have blushed, but I just looked over his face with interest.

"I guess I didn't realize anyone noticed me."

"How could anyone not?"

I dropped my eyes back to his laptop and swigged the last of my coffee. "I should get going."

"Sure. Look, I'm sorry if I made you uncomfortable. That wasn't my intention."

"You didn't," I reassured him as I stood and gathered the textbooks I'd brought from the table. "I just have some stuff to do today." Yeah, like avoiding Kit before the dinner I was being forced into having with him and my parents.

"Are you and Kit...?"

I froze, looking up at him and then away, out of the window. "It's complicated." That felt like the understatement of the year.

"I can work with that," Harley said slowly, a smile curving

his mouth in a way I might have really appreciated if I hadn't already been caught up on someone else.

I opted to say nothing, just gave him a slight smile as I grabbed my to-go cup and dropped it in the trash as I headed for *Cocoa & Rum's* door.

Harley was nothing and everything like I'd expected. I was happy he seemed to like me, but for all the wrong reasons. If he was into me, then that meant he probably wasn't into Kit. I had no right to feel possessive, but logic didn't stop the feeling anyway.

I decided to stroll around the park before heading home so I could clear my head a little. It felt like there was a rubber band stretched taut between Kit and me right now and at any given moment it could snap. I didn't want to feel the sting, I didn't want the burn. If I could have gone back in time and not told that white lie to my mother, maybe I would have done it.

But then you'd never have known what it was like to have him be yours, an insidious little voice insisted in my head and I glowered at the sky from the bench I had stopped to sit on.

"Leo?"

I nearly jumped, so lost in my thoughts I hadn't noticed anyone approaching. It was Ryan, now our sole captain of the football team after we'd had Aaron kicked out for doing drugs. Not that it mattered much really, the season was over now, but it was the principle of the thing I supposed.

He was by himself, which felt like a rarity these days. I'd become used to seeing Jamie at his side, like a dark-haired devil attached to his hip.

"Hey man." I stood as he closed the distance and smiled. The deepness of the blue sky made Ryan's eyes pop even more than usual, the Clark Kent resemblance he bore out in full force. "Where's your worse-half today?"

Ry grinned, knowing I was teasing. "Recording studio with Max. Kit back at your place?"

I nodded. "Yeah, he's keeping my parents entertained while I tutored a guy from class."

"Ah, cool. How long are they down for?"

"Barring any more car trouble, they should be leaving tomorrow."

Ryan's dark brows drew together as he watched me before his expression cleared. "Car trouble, huh. Well, I'll see you on Tuesday then?"

I nodded and he smiled before walking away. Something about the way he'd looked at me seemed... off. I couldn't put my finger on what it was, but it was like he'd had a realization of some kind. About what, I had no idea.

I made it home without seeing anybody else and I was grateful for that fact. My small-talk battery had been almost completely drained. I needed somewhere quiet to recharge.

I could hear my mom talking in the kitchen and decided to wait a bit before going in so I didn't have to see whoever else was in there chatting with her. Instead, I nudged open Kit's door and flopped into his bed after nudging off my shoes. It still smelled like him and my body relaxed as I pushed my hands through my hair, massaging my scalp. It was nice that my family had come to visit, but I wasn't built for so much socialization day after day. Plus with dinner tonight... I needed to take a moment for myself, to just close my eyes and sit there quietly. The next thing I knew, I was being nudged awake by gentle hands.

"Hey," Kit said softly and I blinked, confused about where I was and why he was waking me up. "You should probably get up now if we want to make the dinner with your parents."

Dinner. Shit. Had I really slept that long? "I'm sorry, I didn't mean to sleep for so long—"

"It's okay, I get it. But I thought you might want to wake yourself up a bit before we leave." Kit stood, pulling away from the edge of the bed where he'd been crouched. "How was tutoring with Harley?"

"Good," I said and then considered, thinking back to everything he'd said. "And weird."

"How so?"

I shrugged. "Just some of the things he says."

"Like what?"

Was it just me, or were Kit's words more clipped than usual? "He asked about us."

Kit stilled, his back to me as he considered the contents of his cupboard and then tugged his tee up and over his head, the corded muscles in his back flexing with the movement. "Oh? And what did you tell him?"

I swallowed hard as I followed the line of his spine down to the beginnings of his jeans. "That it's complicated."

I got the feeling that I'd said the wrong thing almost immediately.

"Right."

"Kit—" I tried and he spun around, buttoning his short-sleeved gray shirt up and over his abs.

"We have to leave soon or we'll be late," he said curtly and stalked out of the door, leaving me sitting up in his bed, open-mouthed.

It didn't seem to matter what I said when it came to Harley, just saying his name was enough to piss Kit off.

I quickly freshened up and threw on a clean shirt—one my mom had got me in a deep forest green. I didn't wear it often because it tended to cling to my shoulders and was a little too tight in the neck, so I had to wear the first few buttons open.

Kit turned to face me as I jogged down the stairs, mouth opening like he was going to say something and then shutting when his eyes dropped to my shirt. He cleared his throat and I let him stew, reluctant to be the first to break the silence considering he had been the one to storm away. *Anyone would think he was my real boyfriend.* I wanted to laugh at the thought, but it mostly just depressed me—it seemed like all kinds of desperate to want your fake boyfriend to be fake jealous.

"You missed a few buttons," he said eventually and stepped in close to me as I finished tying my laces. I opened my mouth to respond, to tell him it was deliberate, but no sound came out as his warm hands brushed the skin of my throat and his fingertips ghosted across my chest.

I caught his hands in mine and his eyes flew up, his breaths coming faster and feathering across my mouth in a way that was dizzying. I tugged the buttons open again and his eyes slid closed. "It's too tight if I do them all up."

"Right." Kit's voice sounded strange, almost hoarse, and his eyes were still screwed shut as the muscle in his jaw popped.

"Are you okay?" I instinctively caught his chin in my palm as I dropped his hands, tugging his head towards me so I could look at him more closely. "Do you need some water or something?" Eyelids lifted and deep blue eyes filled with heat froze me in place before I dropped my hand from him like I'd been burned. "Maybe we should just get going," I said hastily and a small smile passed over his face.

Kit gestured towards the door and I carefully stepped around him, aware of every inch of space between us and how quickly it could be breached.

"*Giorgio's?*" I guessed when we turned towards the mall rather than the direction of *Cocoa & Rum* and Kit nodded. It was probably the nicest place to eat that we had in Sun City, if you wanted to eat something other than a burger or salad. "Thanks for doing this," I said quietly as we walked and Kit raised a dark eyebrow in my direction. "The extra day of the boyfriend package," I explained, trying to smile and failing. He said nothing and it unnerved me. Kit was never usually lost for words—if anything, he was the one who felt compelled to fill the silence.

It was early enough that birds were still flitting in and out of the trees we walked underneath and people still lounged on the grass, soaking up the last of the sunshine for the day. It should have been a pleasant walk. Instead, I felt sick.

"It's just so strange," I rambled. "My dad's meticulous about his car, especially when it comes to long journeys. But I'm glad to see them for the extra day, though—" I glanced up at Kit quickly and then sharply away when I found him watching me. "—I'm obviously sorry it meant another day of pretending for you."

"I don't mind," he said easily and I tried not to sigh. It wasn't that I thought he was lying, but Kit was nice enough to try and spare my feelings.

I didn't bother replying, just tried to keep breathing steadily as the greenery passed by, inhaling the smell of freshly-cut grass and breathing out my anxiety like it was a physical thing I could release.

A hand caught mine and I looked down in surprise, a kernel of warmth growing inside me when Kit didn't let go and instead pulled me closer. I didn't pull away and his fingers tightened around mine for a moment as we walked, the silence suddenly feeling less oppressive.

This was our final night together as an *us* and I still hadn't figured out whether or not Kit had liked being together enough for me to convince him to stay. I wanted him, and it scared me. My mom said the best things in life are normally the things that scare us the most, and that definitely rang true when it came to Kit.

Giorgio's was relatively quiet considering we were nearly at the end of the week—though admittedly it was the kind of place you took your parents or a date, so it wasn't usually as packed as *The Box* or *Cocoa & Rum.*

My parents were already waiting at a table in the center of the hall and I looked longingly at the more secluded booths that lined the windows. I hated being seated so out in the open where the server could lean over and get in my personal space without warning. What alarmed me most, however, was the pretty top my mom was wearing and the faint hint of make-up on her eyes and cheeks. My dad, usually forever casual, was in a shirt and that was akin to black-tie for him.

I'd prepared for a nice meal and a night of small talk. My mom caught my eye and her smile said *mischief.* It was a look I'd seen on Saylor too many times before. Fuck. This wasn't some casual *thanks for having us* dinner. This was an interrogation.

"You okay?" Kit murmured as we walked closer and I realized I was probably cutting off the circulation in his fingers.

"I'm sorry for this."

He shot me a raised-eyebrow look of concern before hiding it quickly as we pulled out our chairs and sat down opposite my parents.

"You both look nice," I said sourly and my mom grinned.

"Thank you, sweetie. I feel like we've barely had any time to speak to you with all the sight-seeing we've been doing, so I thought it would be nice to have a proper catch-up."

I narrowed my eyes and my dad had the grace to look a little guilty. Kit's eyes flicked back and forth between my parents and me, blissfully ignorant about what was happening. It had been so long since I'd let my parents meet anyone I was seeing that I'd forgotten how my mom tended to react.

"Of course," my mom continued, "it's been nice getting to know you better too, Kit. Tell me, how did you and Leo meet?"

"Mom," I said warningly, trying to head her off when Kit's mouth turned up in a half-smile.

"You know, I'm not sure I remember. It feels like Leo's always been there, by my side."

A strange sensation swooped in my belly and I kept my eyes fixed straight ahead, not wanting him to see anything in my eyes that might give away how he made me feel in that moment.

"Football," I said softly. "Through the team."

"And you were friends for a while first?"

"Yes," I gritted out and was relieved when the server came over to take our drink order, offering a brief reprieve.

"And after college, once you both have your degrees, what then?" My mom continued once the server had walked away.

"Mom," I protested and she blinked her eyes innocently at me.

"What? It's not like this is a brand new relationship, Leo. You need to think about these things! I don't want either of you getting your heart broken because you thought this relationship is something it wasn't."

I sat back, surprised. She'd *never* been this defensive before. What was different? "It's our relationship, Mom. We'll figure that out together. It's got nothing to do with you."

"Leo..." my dad said, a warning clear in his tone and I bit my tongue for a moment before releasing a slow breath.

"I'm sorry, I appreciate your concern. But I don't need you to worry about my relationship—or interrogating my boyfriend." The words made my stomach tumble for a second. Was it the first time I'd said those words aloud?

"Oh," Kit said, laughing, but his eyes were full of a languid heat that made me swallow as he looked first at me and then to my parents. "That's what this is—you want to know my intentions towards your son. It's very honorable."

"Well?" my mom said and I groaned.

"I love him," Kit said and the words were like a balm and a blade in one. "Wherever he goes, I'll follow. Whenever he needs me, I'll be there. And if I'm lucky enough, he'll let me do all of that forever."

Too much. It was too damn much.

I pushed back from the table abruptly and nearly walked into the waitress carrying our drinks. "Restroom," I muttered as I hurried away from the table, head spinning and mouth too dry and yet somehow filled with saliva. God, I was going to hurl.

They were the perfect words. Words that, under any other circumstances, I would have died to have heard from his lips. I wanted them to be true more than anything. But they weren't, and the fact that he could say them so convincingly, without even blinking, made me feel worse. Did I really mean so little to him that the lie came easily?

The door to the restrooms swung open with force as I pushed my way inside to find it blissfully empty. I strode for one of the stalls, locked the door, and sat down on the closed lid, my face in my hands. My breaths were too quick and my hands trembled against my cheeks, pressing hard into my eyes like I could somehow erase the image of him sitting next to me, saying those things.

I wasn't a violent person, but the urge to punch something was riding fierce inside me, leaving me feeling drained. How was I supposed to go out there and smile, nod, like it didn't hurt to breathe when I wasn't around him? That the thought of us going separate ways after Sun City didn't fill me with an unprecedented level of terror?

I pushed out a breath and then another, trying to calm my thoughts down, trying to ignore the memories pressing in on me of the taste of Kit's mouth and the feel of his hand in mine.

"Leo?"

I held my breath. Kit.

"Leo, I know you're in here. Why are you hiding from me?"

"I'm not hiding," I said through the door. "I'm... using the facilities."

"No, you're not." I wasn't. "You don't use public restrooms."

Fuck. Why did he have to know me so well?

I stood abruptly, that same anger washing over me in a ceaseless wave of red that made dampness gather on my lashes as I bit my lip so hard I tasted blood.

The scrape of the lock was loud and grating but I barely heard it as I charged towards him. His blue eyes were wide, concerned, and that only infuriated me more. My hands moved of their own accord, sliding into his hair as I stepped closer, our breaths joining as the heat from his lips taunted me like a threat. I set my jaw.

"What the hell is wrong with you?"

Kit stepped back and my hands fell to my side. "With *me*?"

"I feel like I don't even know you. How could you say those things to her?"

For once, Kit looked speechless. Mouth parted, eyes wide, hands limp at his side he shook his head slightly. "I'm sorry. I didn't realize it would upset you so much. You know our friendship is the most important thing to me and I wouldn't ever do anything to compromise that."

In other words, maybe he did find me attractive. But he wouldn't act on those feelings beyond this ruse because when all was said and done, Kit only saw me as a friend.

"You didn't have to take it this far," I said quietly. Not because my anger had faded, but because it had left me bone tired. "You didn't have to make her think..." I shook my head. The jealousy, the lies, the casual touches and laughter and, god, the way he always seemed to know what was on my mind—all of it had screwed with my head. "I think it might be too late to worry about our friendship. I told you," I said, lowering my eyes to the ground so his wouldn't keep burning into mine. "This was a bad idea from the start." Because I didn't think I could go back to loving him distantly—and it was love. I could admit it freely now. I wanted more than friendship from my best friend, and that wasn't fair to him or me.

I walked away, back out of the bathroom and to the table in a daze. My parents were chatting together as they looked over the menu and I watched them dully as I approached. We hadn't even made it to the entrees.

I sat down opposite them and smiled when my dad asked if everything was okay. It wasn't. It really fucking wasn't. And tomorrow, my parents were leaving and I wasn't sure if Kit would still be there when they did—or if I even wanted him to be.

The chair next to me slid back and Kit sat down. I avoided his eyes, instead focusing on my parents debating what to order. Tomorrow, everything would be different.

They managed to get through the remainder of the meal without much drama, but I couldn't relax. Tension radiated out of Kit at my side and when he reached for my hand during the walk home, I pulled it back to point at something random in the distance while chatting to my parents. I had to start distancing myself. If I wanted to have any chance of getting back to some semblance of normal with Kit, then I never should have let myself get carried away. That meant no more kissing, or touching.

Or sharing the bed.

Kit was silent as I rolled up a blanket and grabbed my pillow from his bed. Our breaths filled the room and somehow it was worse than the silence, knowing the other was there and yet what was there left to say?

I rolled over again, trying to get comfortable, when he sighed.

"Jesus, Leo. Take the bed. I'll go stay with Xander."

I opened my mouth to respond but the bed dipped and the door shut quietly before I could get any words out. In the darkness, the scent of him wrapped around me, I was sure that love had never cut this sharp before.

CHAPTER NINE

I'D WAVED GOODBYE TO MY PARENTS THAT MORNING and had genuinely been sorry to see them go—and not just because things with Kit felt awful.

We were polite, courteous, and entirely pleasant with each other, but it felt like we were walking on a tightrope, one wrong look away from falling. As a result, I'd been in an awful mood with everyone else recently.

Ryan had noticed it during our basketball game on Tuesday and even Xander, who tended to be almost as oblivious as me, had asked me if everything was alright. They were being nice, checking in, but having them all peering at me with concern while Kit was there, face studiously blank and unaffected had been maddening.

I'd carried that bad mood with me still on Wednesday morning when I met up with Harley for another tutoring session. He brought another essay along for me to look at and I'd highlighted something in red so brutally I'd torn through the paper with my pen. I'd reluctantly agreed to meet him at *Cocoa & Rum* because I had been fairly sure Kit wasn't working, but he'd arrived for a shift about ten minutes ago and my mood had worsened with his appearance.

"Leo," Harley said, clearly not for the first time by the slightly exasperated look on his face. "Are you alright?"

"Fine," I said and when he raised his eyebrows at me I sighed. "Just a lot on my mind."

"Well, why don't you come out with me tonight then? They're doing a movie night in the park, blankets, snacks, fairy lights—the works. It's free?"

I thought about it and couldn't see a reason not to go. It would get me out of the house at least and I could stop feeling like my bed was missing something—someone—whenever I was in it. Plus, Harley was... nice. Easy. I didn't have any complicated feelings for him or a history of friendship that was now possibly ruined. I needed to get over Kit. I owed it to myself to try.

"Okay, sure." I handed him his essay back, slightly sheepishly. "Ah, sorry about the hole."

He chuckled and the sound was full of good humor, his eyes sparkling at me. "No worries. I'll text you the details then?"

"Yeah, thanks. See you tonight."

I stood up and cursed as I bumped into something hard behind me. Kit.

"Hi."

There was a muscle ticking in his jaw but he smiled at me brightly. "Big date?"

I shrugged and Kit nodded slowly.

"Cool. Well, I have to get back to work." But there was something in the tightness of his lips, the frown of his eyebrows, that told me if things had been frosty before then they were even chillier between us now.

No. I needed to move on. We needed to just... get this

attraction between us out of our systems for good and then never speak of it again.

I gripped the shoulder strap of my bag tightly as I followed Kit, catching the swinging *employees only* door with my other hand.

He turned to me, an unreadable emotion on his face. I took the first step forwards and the fire in his eyes made me think I was the one aflame.

"What are you doing back here, Leo?" There was a dangerous silkiness to his voice and I knew we were at a breaking point.

I'd been firm. Resolved in my plan to just sleep with him and finally move on, to get my fill and then forget about it. But actually standing there in front of him, I felt my hands shake.

"Nothing," I muttered and then scurried back through the door. Fuck. I probably looked like an idiot. What was the right thing to do in this situation?

I nudged my phone out of my pocket and winced as I opened my messages. Three unread voice notes from Kat. She knew I hated them, especially because she tended to ramble, but I couldn't deny that I needed her advice now. Desperately, if the past five minutes were any indication.

There was an employee-only bay around the back of *Cocoa & Rum* where the employees sometimes took their breaks and I hurried out of the coffee shop and around to it. Moving felt good, like I was tricking my brain into thinking I was doing something to solve the problem when, in reality, I was just as hopeless now as before.

I was pacing. I couldn't get the rich blue of Kit's eyes, deepened by his hair, out of my mind. I wanted him. He wanted me. Neither of us wanted to risk losing our friendship, but I really wasn't sure there was much left to save. If anything, this might be what we needed to do if we wanted to move on.

I was strong enough to admit I loved him, had probably loved him for a very long time if I was being wholly honest with myself. Kit cared about me, I knew that. But whatever had been building between us while my parents had been in Sun City had been less about love and more about lust. *Want.*

I tugged my phone back out of my pocket again and bit my lip before hitting dial.

"...Why would you call me?"

My steps faltered for a second before I resumed pacing around the concrete, my feet scuffing the ground as I walked. "Because I needed to talk to you?"

"God, next time just text me or send a voice message like a regular human."

I rolled my eyes but decided not to push the issue. "Kat. "

"What?"

"I think I'm going to sleep with Kit."

"You've been sleeping with him for ages, right? Your parents had your room. Is this some kind of friendship-memory test?"

I cut her off before she could continue babbling. "No. I mean *sleep* with him."

"Ohhh." She chuckled and I frowned, not wanting her to laugh at me. "You're going to fuck."

"Kat," I protested and she laughed again.

"Sorry, sorry.. Okay. Why is that reason for you to call me?"

"Am I making a mistake?"

The other end of the line went silent as she thought about my question and I appreciated that she actually took the time to think about it before answering.

"I think as long as you both have clear boundaries and understanding about what's happening and what it does or doesn't mean, then you're not making a mistake."

"It's just sex," I said immediately and then froze as the back door opened and Kit stepped outside. "I have to go."

"Wait, I want to know the detai-"

I hung up and met Kit's eyes. "How much of that did you hear?"

"Enough," he said as he closed the door behind him. "Are you going to run away again?"

"No," I said after a moment of hesitation. "It's rude to eavesdrop," I pointed out and he chuckled.

"Is it really eavesdropping if the person talking is somewhere they shouldn't be?" Kit leaned back against the wall, right next to the sign declaring the space only for use of employees.

"Yes."

His foot dropped down and he took a step towards me as I held very still. "We're finally going to do this then?"

"Kit. We need some rules."

"Not much of a fan of rules."

"I need to make sure we're on the same page about what this is," I said breathlessly as his hand fisted into my hair and tugged.

"I know what this is." His voice was hard, but his lips were soft as they brushed the shell of my ear. "I heard you loud and clear. Just sex."

I nodded weakly as he sucked at the skin of my neck. I was painfully hard just from this, his touch, his mouth, and when he pulled away I nearly whimpered.

"I want you to say it, Leo."

"What?"

"Tell me what you want from me."

I swallowed before taking a step closer to him. "I want you to fuck me."

He smiled and it was a slow seduction. "Good. I don't want you to hold back when I make you come for me."

"That's bold of you," I said, struggling to keep my voice steady as my mind whirled. This felt unreal, like I could have been dreaming. "Because I'm going to have you begging in the next five minutes."

His eyes flashed and my breath caught as he closed the last remnants of space between us and cupped my jaw. "I look forward to it."

Our lips met in a clash of tongues and teeth that made me groan, craving more of the taste of him. I bit his lip and he sucked in a breath, his hands curling in my hair before letting go and running across my shoulders and chest.

I knocked his hands away and backed him up towards the wall before kissing him roughly, loving the sounds he made as we learned each other's mouths. I took the bottom of his navy shirt in my hands and tugged until the buttons popped open and I kissed my way from his neck to his chest. Doing this in public seemed like a very bad idea, so I was relieved when he pulled back and guided me through the door to the back of the coffee shop, pushing me into a storage closet and using a mop to hold the door closed.

Then our lips met again, feverish with pent-up desire. He was ridiculously warm and he smelled like summer, sunshine and sweetness. I dropped down and licked a long line from his chest to his navel as he panted, leaning against the door as if for support.

I reached his jeans and my fingers shook as I opened his fly, eager to please him.

"No underwear," I said roughly, palming him as his cock tried to spring out.

"You're welcome," Kit said breathlessly around a laugh.

I stroked him firmly and that made him shut up, his head falling back against the door as his eyes slid shut. I felt like a god with him like putty in my hands, waiting to moan, willing to let me do whatever I wanted.

I dipped my head down to taste him, letting my tongue run

across his underside before looping around to suck his head into my mouth. He was still sweet even here, just with a smokey undercurrent that had me reaching down to free my own cock from my pants as I moaned my appreciation.

I closed my hand around myself as I worked Kit with my mouth, taking him to the back of my throat and flicking his head with my tongue as I withdrew. Soon I had set a pace that had him panting, then pleading with me, and the delicious sounds of his moans made my hand speed up around my cock.

"Leo, Leo," Kit groaned.

I stopped teasing him, hollowing my cheeks out as I sucked and gagging a little as I swallowed him. I jumped when his hand found my shoulder, pushing me away.

"No, I want this to last." His cheeks were pink and a light sheen of sweat made his chest glisten as he pulled me up from my knees and kissed me. "If you keep doing that, this will be over before it really starts."

I smirked but it quickly faded when his hand reached for me, replacing my own.

"I think we need to focus some attention on you for a bit, okay?"

I nodded, my breath stuttering as Kit's hand worked torturous circles over me, until I felt taut with pleasure, dancing on the edge for him.

I sagged against his chest, panting as the warmth of him threatened to undo me. Of course, that was when he stopped, leaving me frustrated until I realized he just wanted to remove more clothes—which I didn't have a problem with.

He stripped off his open-shirt and I followed suit, both of us removing our clothing as quickly as possible, frantic to get back to each other. But once it was done and I stood bare, I couldn't help but stop to look at him. Hours working out and playing for the team meant Kit's muscles were carved perfection. His thigh muscles flexed as he reached down to stroke himself and the hollowed out space in between his hip and his ass begged me to bite it. I'd seen him naked before, of course, in the showers after a game usually, but this was different. This time, I could look my fill.

His gaze was devouring my body just as I drank him in, until a smile touched his lips. "You're gorgeous."

"So are you," I said honestly. "Kit, it's... it's been a while for me. Since I..."

He nodded, the heat in his eyes not dulling even as his face softened. "We'll take it as slow as you need."

I nodded and stepped toward him, feeling suddenly shy, like the fervor had left me and now I was left with the clear-headed realization that this was happening. Kit and me. We were really going to do this.

His arms came around me and I shivered, despite not feeling the cold air. As soon as Kit's lips brushed over mine, any feeling of nervousness faded. This was *Kit*. I never needed to be worried with him.

He pulled back to look at me and nodded slightly, like he'd read my body and wanted me to feel safe.

This time when our lips met it was with hunger driving us, his tongue coaxing mine as our chests brushed against one another. He reached for my cock at the same time that I reached for his and I let out a small laugh that quickly turned into a moan as we taunted each other. God, we probably needed to make more of an effort to be quiet unless we wanted to get caught by the dark-haired girl working the register.

We moved to the ground and I felt wild, untamed, the hardwood floor cold against my skin as I rocked my hips restlessly. My cock twitched watching him crouch between my legs. Moisture glimmered at his tip and I licked my lips, wanting to taste him again, but the time for teasing was done.

Kit reached for his discarded jeans and snagged a condom from his wallet and I groaned. "Shit. We don't have any lube."

He looked to the shelf to my right and I raised an eyebrow when he blushed. "Don't judge, okay? But this closet has seen a lot of action in the past so I just..." He reached behind a bucket filled with paper cups and pulled out a bottle of lube. Right then, I couldn't think through my relief to be disturbed by the thought of how many other people had fucked in this exact spot. "Are you... prepared?"

I tried not to blush and failed when I nodded.

He licked his lips, knowing what it meant considering I'd already told him it had been a while for me. "When did you do it? After I made you come before?"

His voice was low, but my pulse raced.

"Yes."

"God, Leo."

I flushed harder, unable to help myself when he said my name like that, desire pressing down on me so heavily I could barely breathe. Now he knew how long I'd been wanting this, how much I'd hoped this would happen even against my better instincts.

Kit spread the lube it over himself before coming back down to his knees and slipping one lubed finger over my ass and pressing it inside.

I jolted, loving the pressure. It had been too long.

Kit withdrew before adding a second finger to my ass, coating me thoroughly in lube as his cock throbbed against my thigh. I gasped in a breath as he shifted, sliding against me but not pushing in, letting the anticipation build.

I inhaled deeply and released it as he pushed into me, the burn familiar and the ache so sweet.

"Leo," Kit gasped and I rocked my hips into him, telling him I was okay. He growled my name again, pressing my thighs open wider as he pulled me in close, burying his cock inside me even as he reached to stroke me. This felt surreal. I was me and he was Kit, and yet somehow here we were, fucking on the floor in the backroom at *Cocoa & Rum.*

The dual sensation of his thrusts and his hand working my cock made me tense, worried this would end too soon, but he just leaned down and kissed me.

"Don't worry, I won't let you come yet."

My hands grasped his shoulders as he moved over me, the friction sending bursts of color behind my closed lids as I moaned for him.

"Kit—" I gasped and then opened my eyes in irritation when he pulled out of me. "Why?"

"Turn over."

I scowled but obeyed. He had known how close to the edge I had been and, truthfully, I wasn't ready for this to end. Not yet. I wasn't sure I ever would be.

Glad to have my face hidden against the ground so Kit couldn't read my thoughts straight off it, I pressed my ass upwards toward him and reached down to stroke myself as I heard the bottle of lube being set down again.

I'd thought he'd been giving me everything before, but now his pace was driving, bordering on punishing, as his hands clasped my waist from behind and I felt it when he twitched inside me.

My hands grabbed at the floor uselessly as I let him take control, and when he hoarsely said my name, I knew it was time.

Kit thrust into me three more times, his hips circling into mine before he called for me and my climax happened at the same moment, hitting the wood beneath me.

I slumped, exhausted but mindful of the wet patch, and laid there for a moment while Kit tore something behind me and the irritating scratch of a paper towel moved along my ass and back.

I got to my knees, my body aching, and accepted some paper for the floor before getting dressed slowly. I could see my face in the reflection of a shiny piece of equipment, probably spare parts for the coffee machine. It felt like someone else was looking back at me—someone with swollen lips, puffy from kisses, and red marks across his neck, chest, abdomen and lower from the slight stubble on Kit's face. I looked like I'd been thoroughly fucked, but wasn't that what I'd asked him for?

I felt relaxed, but somehow more nervous now than before we'd done...everything. We'd agreed to just sex. Just this one time, to get it out of our system. Just one taste so we could move on. So why did it feel like everything had changed?

"I, um, should probably let you get back to your shift," I said as Kit finished getting dressed.

"Sure." Kit watched me with an unfathomable expression on his face, the coolness returning to his words like the past half hour hadn't happened.

"Okay then," I murmured and left the room as quickly as possible while shooting off a quick message to Kat.

We were wrong. I think I made a terrible mistake.

This was awful. I didn't say-so to Harley, but I honestly couldn't see how anyone would enjoy this. No wonder it was free.

Some time-travel classic from the eighties was playing on the big screen and despite the speakers being turned way up, I had no idea what the actors were saying amidst the chatter, rustling of bags, and even someone's music at one point.

How anyone was supposed to know what was going on was beyond me—they didn't even have the subtitles on. I was halfway to regretting keeping my promise to myself and going out on the date with Harley after what had happened with Kit, and not just because I couldn't get him out of my head.

"You okay? You're frowning," Harley said and I immediately smoothed out my expression.

"Oh, yeah. Just wondering how I've never been to one of these before," I lied and he grinned.

"It's definitely a unique experience."

I hummed my agreement but honestly, I was bored. I tried to focus on the movie, or at the very least the way the sunset was dripping behind the trees. It was gorgeous. Romantic even. It was warm out and Harley had brought us a blanket to sit on and some popcorn to share. With the breeze gently caressing my skin, sitting under the fading sunlight, romance was still the furthest thing from what I was feeling.

"You know, I really appreciate you helping me out with the exam prep."

"Of course," I said easily and then blinked as I realized how close he was sitting to me.

"I was wondering if you wanted to do one more session on Friday morning? Get our heads in the game for the exam in the afternoon?"

"Yeah that sounds good. We can meet at mine and walk over to the exam hall together if you like."

"It's a date," he said with a wide grin that showed off his straight, white teeth glowing faintly against the warmth of his summer tan.

It's an exam, I thought but didn't say. I wasn't interested in him in a romantic way. He was nice enough, but my head was somewhere else. With *someone* else. Even if I wished that wasn't the case.

My phone buzzed in my pocket and my eyebrows rose when I retrieved it to find Kat, of all people, calling me.

"Why are you calling me?" I said, mimicking her reaction from earlier that day.

"Leo, can you come and meet me? It's important." She didn't sound distressed, exactly, but she wasn't her normally chirpy self either.

"Of course, *The Box*?" I asked and Harley looked up at me, brows furrowed.

"Yeah, see you soon. And Leo? Thank you."

I hung up, feeling more than a little worried about what was going on with her. "I'm really sorry but I have to go. One of my friends needs me."

Harley smiled. "It's alright, I get it. I'll see you Friday, then?"

I nodded and stood, brushing off my jeans for any stray bugs or grass that had snuck onto the blanket. Luckily I wasn't that far from *The Box* so it would only take me a few minutes to get from the center of the park to the strip of bars around the corner from Jamie and Liv's place.

The sun had almost fully gone down by the time I got to *The Box* and slid into the booth opposite Kat. She looked a little frazzled, her curly hair more frizz than the sleek curls she normally wore, and her mascara was slightly smudged under her eyes like she'd fallen asleep with it on.

"What's wrong? Is everything okay?"

The smile she gave me lacked its usual punch and that had a pit forming in my stomach.

"Yes. No. I don't know, honestly."

"Tell me," I demanded and she took a long pull on whatever drink was in her glass before opening her mouth again.

"I got the contract."

"For what?"

Her eyes bugged out. "The marriage, Leo. You know, the one we're semi-faking."

"Semi?"

"Well, it'll be a real, legal marriage. But we're not like, in love or anything." She looked away from me as she spoke the words and I frowned.

"So you want me to look over the contract?"

"Yes, but I just... He wants me to meet his parents and from his description of them, they're absolute a-holes. What if this doesn't work? What if they realize we're faking?"

I shrugged. "It doesn't matter. Their stipulation for Max is that he be married, right? As long as there's no clause or specifications about them having to approve then I don't see what the problem would be. Unless... you care?" There she went again, avoiding my eyes. I folded my arms across my chest. "You never did tell me how you guys met, or how this whole deal was arranged."

Kat said nothing, slurping noisily on her drink instead.

The fact that she wouldn't tell me told me everything I needed to know.

"You slept together."

"Just the one time," she protested, the words practically bursting out of her. "We were both drunk, he was sad and pissed at his parents. I'm always mad at mine so I commiserated, one thing led to another..."

"And now you're getting married," I finished for her and she winced.

"Could you just take a look at this please and make sure I'm not signing away my soul?"

She slid over a bundle of paper and I raised my eyebrows, most contracts were done digitally nowadays. I scanned the document. Most of it was standard prenuptial stuff and I read it aloud to Kat as I went, explaining the terms as she watched me, nibbling anxiously on her bottom lip.

My eyes widened when I got to the part that stated her compensation. "Holy shit."

"I know." She laid her head in her arms on top of the table.

"You're getting a good deal here. Everything looks alright to me, but I'm not a lawyer yet. There's a few local firms you could reach out to just to be sure?"

She shook her head. "I trust you, and I trust Max. Besides, it's supposed to be a secret. So the less people who know, the better. He wants us to 'date' first, so it doesn't come out of the blue for his parents."

"Makes sense," I murmured. "I guess the only thing that's not covered in this," I said, holding up the contract for emphasis, "is your ethical obligations."

"Meaning?"

"You're being tied into a fake marriage for at least a year. You have emotional and physical needs. Is he going to provide for those? Or are you able to seek them elsewhere, so long as you're discreet?"

"Are you asking if I can fuck other people?"

I rolled my eyes. "Yes."

"Hm, I didn't think of that. I guess I'll ask him."

Somehow, I wasn't sure that would go over well, but it was better that they went into the contract with their eyes open.

"So? Are you going to sign it?"

She bit her lip before nodding slowly. "I think so. It's a good deal for me. Max gave me until Friday to decide."

I raised an eyebrow, that didn't feel like much time for such a big decision.

She shrugged, noticing the look on my face. "He's on a deadline. If he doesn't get the funds through in time he'll have to shut down the studio in Sun City."

"Fair enough. Well, it sounds like congratulations are in order."

"They are?" She frowned before blinking at me, a glazed look in her eyes as if this was only just now hitting her. "They are. I'm getting married."

I smiled slightly. "I expect a mention in your wedding toast."

"Oh god. I'm going to have to have a wedding and pick out a dress and bridesmaids and—"

I covered her hand with mine. "One step at a time."

"Right." She blew out a long breath and shook her head as if to clear it. "What were you up to before I called anyway? It sounded noisy."

"I was watching a movie in the park." Kat gave me a look and I sighed, giving up the rest of the info. "With a guy."

"You were on a *date*? And you left?"

"You said it was urgent," I protested and she laughed.

"Oh god, I'm sorry Leo. Was it going well at least?"

I shrugged. "It was fine."

"Does this mean you're moving on from Kit?"

"I don't think I'll ever move on from Kit. It's not that simple."

"Well in that case, I think we should get you a drink."

"Fuck, yes."

CHAPTER TEN

"How was your date with Harley?" Kit asked as he crunched into a near-burnt piece of toast. All three of us were in the kitchen for a change, it felt like we didn't get to say more than a fleeting hello or goodbye now that exam season was coming to a close. But it wasn't like Kit and I were doing much talking lately anyway.

"Fine." I didn't bother to elaborate or tell him it wasn't really a date, more like an experiment or a test that I'd failed. But maybe it was better this way. It would be easier to move on if Kit thought I was seeing someone else.

Xander cleared his throat awkwardly and I rolled my eyes.

"You need to call my sister," I said, shifting the topic as I stared Xander down. "She said she hasn't heard from you since she left." I'd been hoping my sister would stay a few days extra while my parents headed home, but she'd chosen to go back with them, much to my disappointment.

"I didn't know she wanted me to call." His face turned solemn, dark brows furrowing, and I believed him. Xander wasn't hugely self-aware and with girls, he was hopeless.

"Girls always want you to call."

"How would you know?" He snorted and nearly spat orange juice everywhere when he choked.

"Because I have a sister and she wants you to call her. So do it because I don't want to have to hurt you." I gave him my iciest, most pleasant smile and he immediately picked up his phone before leaving the room, mumbling.

"Nicely done," Kit said with a smirk and I relaxed. For a second, everything felt normal again. But then his eyes dropped to my mouth and my breath caught as he leaned over the breakfast bar to wipe the corner of my mouth with his thumb.

"You had a crumb," he said casually, brushing it away and I clenched my jaw.

"Thanks," I ground out and he nodded. "Harley is coming over on Friday morning by the way, so we're going to need the kitchen."

Kit stilled. "He's coming here?"

"Yes."

"Why?"

"Study. Hang out. You know how it is." Maybe I was making my study session out to be more than it was, but it felt good to see some kind of reaction from him other than chilly indifference. Harley was the only one who seemed to bring it out of him. Maybe Kat had been right after all and there was something to this jealousy thing.

A horrible thought crept up on me and my stomach dropped. What if he wasn't jealous that I was seeing Harley but rather that Harley was seeing me? Maybe he wasn't jealous at all and all this tension was just in my head.

"You need to be careful with him."

"Thanks," I said, sarcasm thick in my voice. "Are you going to tell me to be home by nine, too?"

Kit rolled his eyes. "I'm just saying you don't know him that well and he doesn't know you or how to make you feel comfortable."

"I felt plenty comfortable last night," I lied and watched in fascination as a muscle in Kit's jaw jumped. But was it for me? Or *him*?

"Really? And at *Cocoa & Rum* with me, were you *comfortable* then?"

I shook my head, turning to leave. We weren't going to have this conversation. Not now, not ever. For all intents and purposes, he was sticking to our agreement. Just sex. But what I was struggling with was how *easy* he made it look. How was I supposed to look at him and act like I didn't know how he sounded with my name on his lips as he came? Or know intimately the taste of him on my tongue?

"Leo," he growled and I stopped in my tracks.

"I'm sure I was just as comfortable as the other people who've been inside that closet with you," I bit out and was annoyed when he laughed, a low sound that made my body respond despite myself. I stalked for the door before he could say another word and ignored him as he called after me, just closed the front door quietly as I left. I didn't have a place in mind, I just needed to get *away*.

I stood at the entrance to the park on the opposite side of the street and looked down at my phone, debating before I decided to hell with it and hit call.

"Leo?" Harley said and I breathed out, trying to tell myself this wasn't a mistake. That Harley was what I needed, not Kit.

"Hey," I said tonelessly and then cleared my throat. "I'm sorry about last night. Are you free right now? We could grab a coffee?"

God, I was rusty at this. When was the last time I'd asked someone out? Or even cared to?

"I wish I could but I'm actually busy right now. I'll see you tomorrow morning though, yeah?"

"Right. No worries, see you then."

I held the phone to my forehead for a second after I hung up, struggling to work out what I was feeling. Definitely relief. Annoyance. But I wasn't sure if I was more mad at Kit or myself. I'd ruined us single-handedly. How had we even got to this point?

"Leo?"

I jumped and turned to find Bryn, Kit's sister standing behind me. "Oh, hey. You going to see Kit?"

She nodded but scanned my face with eyes so much like her brother's it hurt my heart a little. "Yeah I was. But are you okay?"

I shrugged. "I honestly don't know."

Bryn nodded toward the park and then took my arm in hers when I didn't make a move towards it. "You guys messed things up, huh."

I grimaced. "I don't know what we did, but there's no undoing it."

"Do you love him?"

I looked at her in surprise before nodding slowly and she smacked me on the arm.

"You're both such idiots. Maybe you don't need to undo anything—have you thought about that?"

"Bryn, he doesn't want—"

"No, Leo! He *does* want. And so do you! So why are you fighting it so hard?"

I bit my lip before admitting, "I'm scared."

She let the admission settle into the air between us, the sounds of dogs barking and insects chirping replacing any words we might have said before she nodded. "So is he. You have to make a choice."

"Okay," I said hesitantly, tilting my head to watch a cloud drift past so I didn't have to meet her eyes.

"You need to decide if you're going to be the strong one, the brave one, and tell him what you want."

"I don't know if—"

"Or," she said, cutting me off with a sharp look, "you can let him go. It's not fair to either of you to keep torturing yourselves like this. Either tell him what you want, or let him walk away. You can't have both."

"I don't want to lose him," I whispered and was surprised she'd heard me when one long, pale arm draped itself across my shoulders.

"Then you know what you need to do."

I nodded and we sat there in silence, people watching until she stood up. "Are you off to give him the same speech you just gave me?"

She smiled. "Maybe."

I laughed with her but declined going back to the house. I would talk to Kit, but not right now. I needed time to think, to decide the right thing to say.

"Oh, actually, could you do me a favor?"

I raised an eyebrow. "Sure, what is it?"

"I told Kit I would bring over one of his pieces from the art studio for his showcase but I forgot to grab it. Things have been... intense, lately, staying at Jamie's," she added and I winced, nodding sympathetically. Jamie was a bit like a whirlwind, I wasn't sure anyone's life was the same after having her in it.

"Yeah sure, I'll collect it for him now and bring it home with me."

She beamed and I couldn't help but return the smile. "You're a star. Thank you!" Bryn gave me a tight, but brief, hug and then began walking in the other direction of campus with a wave of her hand.

I'd only been to the art studio a handful of times, but I vaguely remembered where it was. Mostly I'd met Kit there after class, seeing as I had no reason to be in that part of campus. My course was a lot less creative than Kit's.

The journey was relatively short and I was close to overheating by the time I arrived, the main problem with being so fair-skinned. The AC was set to full-blast and I exhaled roughly, enjoying the feeling of it across my sweaty body and face. The corridors were long, carpeted in a strange teal color that somehow managed to look flat and faded instead of cheerful—like being at a doctor's office. There was a large classroom at the end of the corridor that I knew they stored the pieces for showcases in, I'd been with Kit one time to drop a piece off. I'd actually almost forgotten that he had another showcase coming up. I never usually missed one but I'd been distracted lately with surprise visits and exams and... sex with my best friend.

I found the right room and stopped dead at the sight of all the racks in front of me. How the hell was I supposed to find Kit's piece among all this? I started to wonder if Bryn knew what this room held in store and had forgotten on purpose to avoid it. I really couldn't blame her.

I walked down the first of the mini corridors, examining the various cubby holes for Kit's name—it wasn't even in alphabetical order and my palms itched at the thought of getting in there and organizing this whole thing.

I wasn't sure how much time had passed when I heard a rustle at the door and looked up over the chest-high stacks to see Kit staring at me, eyes wide.

"Kit?"

"Leo?" he said at the same time and we chuckled awkwardly. "What are you doing here?"

"Bryn said you had a piece for your showcase here that you asked her to collect and she forgot, so I said I'd do it for her. Why are you here?"

Kit squinted like he was doing really hard math and I bit my lip on the smile I could feel trying to form. "Bryn said she'd seen my professor in the park on her way to me and that I needed to label a couple of my pieces before they got lost." He shook his head, blue hair falling over on eye. "Did she parent-trap us?"

"I think so," I said, half-laughing around my sigh as I walked over to him, twisting my hands together so I would reach for his hand. It had only been a few days, but I'd started to get used to the casual touches we'd used around my parents. They'd felt natural, like it seemed strange that we had spent so long *not* doing that. "I guess I'll head home, then."

"Leo," Kit said as I started to walk past him. "Can we talk?"

I squeezed my eyes shut for a moment before nodding stiffly.

Kit led the way out of the room, leading us into an art room that had been haphazardly slapped and speckled with paint, likely as people worked on their pieces. The riot of color actually relaxed me though–it reminded me of Kit.

He sat down at a table and gently nudged a chair out from under it with his foot so I could sit too. "I just feel like, lately we've been at odds. Normally we're so in sync that I forget that there are times when we're not on the same page—and I feel like there's been a lot of that recently. So I'm sorry."

He wanted to talk about our communication? "It's okay."

"No," he insisted, "it's not. I should have told you then and I don't know why I didn't, I guess you pissed me off." He grinned and I raised an eyebrow, confused about what he was saying. "I meant everything I said to your mom. Every single word. You're my best friend, Leo. You just..." He shook his head. "I meant it. I'm sorry I didn't try to explain better at *Giorgio's*."

He'd meant it? *"I love him. Wherever he goes, I'll follow. Whenever he needs me, I'll be there. And if I'm lucky enough, he'll let me do all of that forever."* "You mean, as a friend?"

Something shuttered in his eyes but he nodded. "Right. Yeah."

I blew out a long breath and rubbed my hand across my face. "It's okay. I'm sorry I blew up at you about it. I guess it just caught me off guard."

We watched each other for a moment before Kit smiled, revealing a flash of his tongue piercing. "So, we're good?"

"We're good," I confirmed and he relaxed. I hadn't even realized how tense he'd been until that moment.

"So you and Harley, huh," he tried and I grimaced.

"Nope, let's not talk about that."

Kit snorted. "Okay. You know, you should really try and talk about things more instead of keeping it all bottled up." He stood and made his way over to a long counter against the wall, long since covered in paint splashes that covered up most of the white. "Or you can do what I do," Kit said, placing a large piece of brown paper in front of me as well as a cup of water, paintbrush, and what looked like watercolors. "And paint instead of talking it out. Sometimes I don't even know what I'm feeling until I have a brush in my hand. Go on. Try it."

His fingertips brushed mine as he passed over the paintbrush. "I don't know how."

"You can't do it wrong," Kit pointed out and I frowned.

"Of course you can."

"That's the beauty of art," Kit rolled his eyes and cupped my hand, encouraging me to dip the brush in the water before picking a paint color, "there are no mistakes, no rules, no confines. You can just be... whatever you want."

What I wanted, I thought but didn't say, was to be his. But this, friendship with him, would have to be enough.

I smiled and he returned it as the tension from the last few days seemed to fade away until things almost felt normal again. Almost.

By the time I got home later that evening, I was wearing an uncomfortable amount of paint. I was desperate for a shower, but as I walked up the stairs, I paused at the sound of giggling coming from Xander's room. He'd said he would call my sister, but now he was in there with some other girl? And what was with all the giggling anyway? Xander wasn't that funny.

I didn't even knock, just pushed open his door, ready to yell at him for leading my sister on, but I stopped short at the sight of a familiar blonde head.

"Saylor?"

My sister turned around and my eyes widened as I took in her position, sprawled atop my roommate. "Geez, knock much?"

"What are you doing here? Why didn't you tell me you'd come back?"

"I wanted it to be a surprise," she said, shrugging one pale shoulder as Xander carefully disentangled himself. I couldn't help but think I'd had enough surprises for a lifetime in the past two weeks.

Saylor stood fluidly and strode over to me, wrapping me in a quick hug before she let go. "I changed my mind about leaving, so I came back."

"How far did you get?" I asked as I leaned in the doorway.

"If you're asking how long it took for me to start missing you, I'm still waiting for it to kick in."

I snorted. Brat. "Okay, well, be safe, behave, etcetera. I'm going to shower."

"Why *are* you covered in paint?" she called after me and I smiled inadvertently.

"I was with Kit."

Kit. Oh shit, did this mean we weren't yet done pretending? And just when things had started to get back to normal... Saylor could be trusted, she wouldn't say anything to Mom and Dad. *Unless she's pissed you duped her too.* Fuck. I was going to have to think carefully about all this, before I did something I couldn't take back or make things with Kit worse.

I sighed as I locked the bathroom door. Why couldn't something just go right for a change?

CHAPTER ELEVEN

MY SISTER HAD BEEN STAYING WITH US FOR TWO days and already I wanted to pull my hair out. She was just so—

"Incorrigible!" I yelled as I glared at my sister, sitting innocently at the breakfast bar munching on *my* cereal, as I held the empty box in my hand. "Seriously?"

"Just have something else," Xander said with a shrug and I ground my teeth.

"It's Thursday."

"So?"

"So—"

"Leo has cereal on a Thursday," Kit said, yawning as he walked into the room and headed for the cupboard, passing me a fresh box of the brand I liked. "Noticed you were getting low so I grabbed you one when I was at the store."

My throat went dry and I blinked several times as I accepted the box. Jesus, was I really getting emotional over cereal?

"Xander and I were thinking about going to a karaoke bar tonight, Kit, do you want to come?" Saylor placed her spoon in the bowl gently and I took it from her, placing it in the sink for later.

"And where's my invite?" I grumbled and Saylor shot me a look.

"Do you want to come to the loud bar filled with people who can't sing, spilling drinks on an already-sticky floor, Leo?"

Smartass. She knew there was nothing I'd hate more—except having to be the one singing, maybe. "Sounds great."

Kit laughed. "Well, I can't come. I have my showcase tonight so I'll be on campus for most of the evening."

"Ah, yes," I said, glancing between the two of them. "Kit's showcase. I also have that to attend. Sorry. So sad to miss out on all the fun."

"Did somebody say fun?" Bryn strolled in and Xander raised an eyebrow.

"How did you get in here?"

"I have a key," Bryn said in her best *duh* voice and I struggled to keep a straight face. "What's this fun you speak of? I can't remember a time of fun, not with exam prep happening."

"Speaking of." I stuck a spoon in my bowl and paused next to Kit, pressing a quick kiss to his cheek and hoping it seemed couple-y enough for Saylor but friend-y enough for Kit. "Thank you for the cereal. I'm going to go study in my room."

"Anytime," Kit murmured and we locked eyes for a moment before I escaped up into my bedroom.

I jolted upright, my eyes flying wide as I fumbled for my phone, desperate to check the time. It was dark outside and worry filled me. Surely I hadn't missed Kit's event. I *never* missed one of

Kit's events. I'd fallen asleep on top of my textbook and it felt like I had one of the pages embedded in my cheek.

"Relax, it doesn't start for another hour," Saylor said gently and I laid back down again, breathing easier and not even questioning why she was in my room.

"You could have led with that instead of letting me panic."

"I *did* lead with that," she said dryly and I rolled my eyes.

"Why did you come back really?" I prodded and she shrugged.

"I don't know. I just felt like I wasn't done here and with my internship wrapped up for now... I just figured I'd do what felt right."

I nodded, accepting that. Saylor had her own mind and I knew she was more than capable of deciding what she wanted for herself. "Are you going to look at any other colleges?"

She shook her head. "I think Mom just wanted an excuse to see you. You know what she's like."

And I did. She was a worrier.

"I think she feels better after seeing you with Kit, knowing you have someone."

That sent a flare of guilt through me, but I just nodded slightly, keeping my eyes on the ceiling instead of meeting the question I could hear in Saylor's voice.

"Kit's great," I said truthfully and she nodded.

"Don't let him get away," she said quietly and I opted not to respond even as my heart sped up. Did she know? "I don't think you'll ever forgive yourself otherwise."

The art department typically held their showcases in the same place every year and today was no exception. The large auditorium had been cleared of the previous year's artwork and new pieces decorated the walls or were propped up on podiums. The chatter in the room made me grit my teeth, the echoes grating along my nerves until I spotted Kit and relief filled me.

The artists hovered next to their stands, ready to take questions or describe their piece, but for the most part people simply walked around and admired what was on display. They'd keep this batch of artwork up until the next showcase, free for other students to come in and explore at any time. It was one of the things I loved most about Radclyffe—they truly loved and valued the arts. I was an appreciator, not a creator like Kit, but I was still proud that unlike so many other colleges in the US, Radclyffe was proud of their creative departments and made them the highlight of their institution.

Sure, Kit and I received some attention for being on the football team and Ryan and Aaron had been on the receiving end of a lot more, but just as many people knew Kit from his art as they did from being on the field.

"Hey," I said in his ear as I stepped up behind him and tried not to smirk when he jumped.

"You're like a cat, you know. I'm thinking about putting a collar with a little bell on you so you can't sneak up on me any more."

I laughed and he smiled as I came to stand beside him. "How's it been so far?"

"Good turn out." Kit flicked his lip piercing with his tongue and I shifted uncomfortably as my body responded. "Have you had a look around yet?"

I shook my head and tried to ignore the way his short-sleeved shirt fit against his shoulders and chest. "Um, no. I wanted to start here with you."

"Honored," he teased and raised an eyebrow when he

looked at me and found my focus on the way the material stretched tightly across his pecs. "Is there something on my shirt?"

I cleared my throat as I quickly reached out and brushed a hand roughly over the smooth material, only a few shades darker than his blue hair. "Lint."

I turned away to the artwork he'd presented on the wall, looking for a distraction, and paused. Kit's work was gorgeous, as always, all clean lines and a chaos of color that somehow fit and melded rather than being overwhelming. But what took me aback was the face in the smaller portrait in the bottom right corner. It was like a pop art style made of multiple coloured lines overlapping to form a familiar outline.

"Is that me?" My voice was hoarse and I clamped down on my emotions as he looked at me, eyes running over my face to try and gauge my response.

"Do you like it?"

"Yes."

"Then yes, it's you." Kit grinned and I lifted my lips in a half-smile. Was this just an artist's eye for an interesting muse? My face was fairly angular, which made it interesting to capture on canvas I was sure, but there was an attentiveness to each feature displayed that made me feel... warm. Seen. "How was your last session with Harley?"

Was it me or was there a distinctly frosty note in his voice? "It was fine. He's smart." I decided not to mention that not only was Harley smart, he was more than a little flirty too. Though he hadn't asked me out again since our date in the park.

"Cool. Good."

We lapsed into a slightly awkward silence and it worried me. Mainly because Kit and I didn't *do* awkward silences. Things had been getting better between us, but Saylor's re-appearance had thrown things off course slightly.

"Relax."

My head snapped toward him in surprise and his eyes on mine were soft. "I can practically feel your brain waves from here. Saylor won't stay forever, and then we don't have to keep up the pretense any more. It'll be okay."

Did he honestly think that *I* was the one suffering here?

"Sure," I said easily and tried to keep my expression from darkening when I spotted Nick in the crowd, heading our way. "I'm sure you're more than ready to get back out there on the scene by now."

Kit looked at me sharply but didn't have time to reply before Nick was in front of us, his beautiful face drawing no small amount of attention from the people around us, like he was a piece of living artwork that had escaped the display.

He greeted Kit and I tuned them out as I searched the crowd for Saylor unsuccessfully, until something Nick said caught my attention.

"Did you guys hear about Jamie's party?"

I held back a groan and Kit's mouth twitched like he knew.

"No, we hadn't heard anything. When is it?"

"Next week. She said something about Ryan putting it in the group chat for you guys, so I'm sure you'll get all the info soon."

"I think I'm busy next week," I said vaguely and Nick chuckled.

"You're going to have to come up with something better than that if you want to convince Jamie."

A flash of white blonde hair struck me and I gritted my teeth into a smile. "Well I'm sure I'll see you then. Be right back," I murmured to Kit and headed off to grab my sister, hoping she would save me from the torture of watching Kit and Nick together.

I guessed I couldn't fault her, she definitely did distract me —but for all the wrong reasons.

I hauled Xander away by the ear and he groaned before shrugging me loose.

"What the hell man?"

"Oh good, your tongue *is* still in your mouth. Only, you were so far down my sister's throat I wasn't sure it could be retrieved."

Saylor rolled her eyes but looked amused as she tidied her smudged lipstick with her pinky finger. It wasn't often I got to play overprotective brother, so she would let me have my fun.

"At least he bought me dinner first," she offered and I shook my head bemusedly.

"Just please don't tell me this is some kind of 'I'm only in town for a small amount of time, take me' thing."

Saylor snorted. "Please. I'm not that desperate for sex."

I grimaced. "I really don't want to know."

Xander didn't look exactly pleased at her words either, which I found interesting.

"Well, I am officially grossed out. So I'll see you later."

Saylor waved cheerily as Xander ignored me, leaning down to murmur something into her ear that made her blush. *Blush.* I tried not to think about it. My sister was as unaffected by things as me most of the time, so I didn't want to devote brain power to what Xander had said to make her look like that.

I wandered the room, inspecting the different artwork on display. Some of it was more graphic-y fine art like Kit's, and others were detailed portraits or sculptures. For a while, I just ignored everything and focused on puzzling out the meanings and emotions behind each piece, until I arrived back at my own face, created with Kit's hands, and found myself unable to look deeper in the same way that I had with the other works. I couldn't trust myself to not see things that weren't there.

Nick and Kit were still talking and laughing together and I would have tried to tamp down the jealousy rising up inside if not for the fact that Saylor was headed this way, probably to say goodbye before they left for karaoke. But for the next few minutes, Kit was *mine*.

I strode over to him and slid my fingers into his, smiling tightly at Nick. His eyes dropped down to my hand intertwined with Kit's and his smile grew bigger.

Frustration rose high in my throat. Did he think that was some kind of challenge?

I tugged on Kit's hand and he turned to me, brows lowered in confusion as he took in my tight jaw. I took his face in one hand and let my thumb brush over his chin before tilting my head and letting my lips seal over his, swallowing his groan like it was better than oxygen.

I kept it brief, not trusting myself to not take it too far if I kept on kissing him like this. I pulled away, trying to slow my rapid breaths as Kit's eyes fluttered open, molten blue beneath his lids.

I glanced casually at Nick and found him talking to my sister, who'd reached us while I'd been kissing Kit.

She turned to us with her trademark smirk of mischief and leaned in close to the white wall where Kit's colorful display featured prominently. "Look Lee-Lee, you're a muse."

I shot her a look and she chuckled as Nick found his way to my side.

"It's about damn time you two fools stopped toeing the line around each other."

I blinked at him, too stunned to voice my thoughts as he nodded in Kit's direction and Kit smiled back.

"I guess we sold it," I offered to Kit as we watched Nick's retreating form.

"Did you invite him here?"

"Who? Nick? Why would I—" But Kit was looking over my head and I jolted in surprise when I saw why.

"Hey guys," Harley said as he walked over to us and Kit smiled but looked more like he was bearing his teeth.

"What are you doing here?" Kit said and I shot him a look as he added, "I mean, I didn't think you liked art."

"I've always been a fan of beautiful things," Harley said as his eyes ran over my face and he stepped closer to Kit. I swallowed as the feeling of being caught like a rope in a tug of war intensified. "Well, I'm going to make the rounds. I'll see you tomorrow?" He said it as if he were addressing the both of us, but his eyes were fixed on mine.

I nodded and he smiled before he walked off. Kit was very still beside me, like he was trying to keep something in.

"You know," he said, turning to look me full in the face, "it's hard for me to make a convincing fake-boyfriend when you're doing whatever it is you're up to with him."

A weird gasp-snort left me as I looked at him. "You're being ridiculous."

"He wants to fuck you," Kit said bluntly and I felt like I wasn't breathing as Kit moved closer.

"So?"

"So?" he repeated before laughing without humor. "You're *mine.*"

"Funny, I don't see your name on me."

He leaned in closer and I shivered as his breath tickled my ear. "I'll happily write it on your damn forehead if that's what it will take."

I pulled back and raised an eyebrow at him, expecting amusement or irritation on his face. Instead, I found desperation.

"Nice," I said, deciding to play things off while I tried to work out what exactly he meant.

Kit pushed a hand through his hair and I watched in fascination. I had no idea what was bothering him so much, but if it was this bad, why didn't he just say whatever it was that was on his mind? "I don't know how else to tell you, Leo. I feel like I'm shouting how I feel in your face and you either don't hear it, or you don't want to listen."

"Shouting what?" I asked, confused and he bit his lip.

"That I don't want to pretend any more!"

I took another step back. "Okay. Then don't. I get it, loud and clear. Alright? I'm going home, I need to study more before my exam tomorrow."

"Leo—"

"Goodnight, Kit. Congrats on the showcase."

CHAPTER TWELVE

"A_RE_ _YOU_ _FEELING_ _NERVOUS_?"

"Maybe a little," I admitted as I leaned across the breakfast bar to make a mark on the essay Harley had brought with him. "I think we're both going to do great though."

"I'll hold you to that prediction," he teased and I smiled. "You make all this look so easy."

I shrugged. "I study a lot."

"I'm not really a fan of books. Or studying."

"Are you sure you want to be a lawyer?" I raised an eyebrow and he laughed before leaning in closer.

"Honestly, I don't know. My parents are the ones who wanted me to study law."

"That sucks," I murmured, focusing on the words in front of me before glancing up and realizing I'd probably sounded callous.

"I mean—"

"No, you're right. It does suck."

The stairs creaked in the hall but I couldn't see anybody

there when I looked up, so I resumed making my notes on Harley's paper while he read over mine.

He let out a low whistle. "You're going to ace this."

"You think?"

"I know," he said, tilting his head so he could peer into my eyes. I jerked up and his smile never faltered. "You know, some people like a guy with a big brain."

I cleared my throat. "Cool."

"I'm definitely one of them," he continued and I didn't know what to say, just kind of nodded. "You know, you're gorgeous Leo."

I should have felt flattered, but I mostly felt irritated. We had an exam in a couple of hours and he wanted to waste valuable study time flirting?

"Thanks," I said shortly and he must have taken that sincerely, because the next thing I knew his hand was under my chin and his mouth was covering mine as he moaned against my lips.

I pulled back just as I heard footsteps in the hall. Kit's silhouette filled the doorway, his face like a thundercloud as he glowered at Harley.

Fuck. This was literally the worst thing that could have happened. I pushed away from the breakfast bar without meeting Kit's eyes. "I'm going to go and grab another textbook from my room," I muttered and Harley smiled and nodded. I brushed past Kit and he caught my wrist, watching me with a level of worry that surprised me.

"I'm okay," I said quietly and he let me go before making his way into the kitchen. I hesitated with my foot on the bottom stair before slowly making my way up, listening hard to hear whatever they might say next.

Kit's voice was pitched low enough that I couldn't make out his words, so I quietly retreated back down the stairs, careful of the one that creaked near the bottom, and listened intently out of sight of the doorway.

"What's your game?"

"I don't know what you mean. I'm here to study."

Kit's laugh was harsher than I'd ever heard from him. "What's your game with Leo? You flirt with him and yet, you watch me."

I heard footsteps and a scrape of a stool as Harley stood and walked to Kit. "Are you jealous?"

"What?"

"Oh come on, don't play dumb Kit. You can't have actually thought I was into *him*. Sure, he's nice to look at, but I've seen more personality from a bag of rocks."

"You were using him." Kit's voice was cold and I peeked around the doorframe to see an unnatural fury on his normally bright face. The truth was that I didn't care what Harley thought of me. I didn't want to hook up with him anyway. But did Kit think I did? Was that why he was so pissed?

"Of course. How else was I supposed to get your attention?"

I moved from my place behind the doorway in time to catch Kit around the waist as he lunged at Harley.

"Don't look at him," Kit hissed as Harley stared at me in shock. "Don't think about him, don't fucking say his name." Kit struggled against my hold and I looked down at him, surprised at how worked up he was.

"I think you'd better go," I said calmly to Harley. "Good luck on the exam."

Harley scooped up his bag and textbooks, shooting one last wary glance at Kit before the front door slammed behind him. As soon as he was out of sight, Kit relaxed in my arms.

"I'm sorry."

"What for?" I asked, genuinely curious.

"For what he said about you," Kit said, eyebrows drawing together as his jaw clenched.

"Not a word of it was true, okay? If he can't see how gorgeous you are inside and out then that's his fucking problem and—"

I kissed him.

Worried about me. Kit had been so mad, because he was *worried about me*. I pulled away, letting him catch his breath as a chuckle escaped my lips. "You're unbelievable."

I stepped away from him and Kit raised his fingers to touch his lips, blue eyes wide as he took me in. "You're not... upset?"

"Why would I be?"

"Because... Harley. I thought you liked him."

"Kit," I said gently, so tired of fighting and pretending. I couldn't do it anymore. Taking his face in my hands, I looked into his eyes. "I'm in love with *you*."

His mouth dropped open and I chuckled again, feeling lighter than I had in days—no, weeks. Bryn, Saylor... they had been right. I had to do what felt right, and this was it. Telling him had been the right thing to do.

"But you—" He shook his head. "You don't care about what he said?"

I snorted. "I couldn't give less of a shit if I tried."

It was like it was all sinking in for him now and I watched as his cheeks turned pink and he sat down heavily in the discarded stool by the breakfast bar.

"You love me?"

"For a long time, now."

"You don't want Harley?"

"Not even a little bit," I said truthfully and his shoulders slumped, alarming me, before he quickly stood and crossed the room.

"Thank god," he said, and kissed me back. It was like he

poured his relief into me, his worry and frustration, and I took it in and gave it all back to him so he could see how much I'd wanted him too.

"Fuck," I pulled away, breathing hard and he grinned breathlessly.

"I know right."

"No, not *that,* although yes the kiss was good. But *fuck* I need to get across the park to campus for my exam."

"Fuck," Kit said, eyes wide and I grimaced, grabbing my bag and shoving things into it before making my way to the door. "We'll talk about this later," he said, but it sounded more like a question.

I nodded. "Of course. Wish me luck."

He stopped me before I could leave, planting a soft kiss on my mouth. "Good luck."

I walked out of the exam room feeling surprisingly good. Given everything that had happened just beforehand, I'd been worried my head would be in another place too completely to be able to focus on the questions. But whether it was the brisk walk, or the calmness that had sunk in after Kit's kiss, my head had felt clear by the time I'd taken my seat and opened my exam paper.

"Leo, can we talk? I'm sorry about before—"

I looked up in surprise to see Harley. I'd assumed he would just brush the whole thing off and act like he wasn't the one in the wrong. Unless he didn't realize how much I'd heard?

"You're not my friend," I said softly, but firmly, and he swallowed. "I have nothing to say to you."

I walked away and was only mildly surprised when he followed.

"I don't know what you think you heard—"

"Don't insult my intelligence. After all, that's the only thing I have, right? Unfortunately a bag of rocks has more personality than me." I stated the words he'd so cruelly thrown out at Kit with zero emotion, watching him with a raised eyebrow. This time when I walked away, he didn't follow.

I shot a quick message off to Kat as I walked back through the park to get home. I'd see her later tonight because we had Jamie's party—something I wasn't particularly looking forward to—but I doubted we'd get much of a chance to speak.

Leo: exam done. Contract signed?

> **Kat:** The paper eagle has left the nest

Leo: ???

> **Kat:** ...Yes. Want to be my maid of honor?

Leo: No

> **Kat:** Fair enough

Leo: I kissed Kit. He nearly punched Harley

> **Kat:** !!! I need more details

Leo: Those are the details?

> **Kat:** You're the worst

I chuckled as I walked, looking up from my phone as I reached the house and finding Kit had tidied away the remaining mess on the breakfast bar. I dropped him a text with a thank you and he responded with a smiley face that made butterflies stir in my stomach. I scoffed at myself.

Damn, I had it bad.

CHAPTER THIRTEEN

KIT HAD BEEN OUT MOST OF THE DAY AND JAMIE'S party took up most of our evening before we could make an escape. Nick had shown up and the spark of jealousy I'd felt when he'd spoken to Kit had actually been somewhat minimal. Liv had wound up being invited to one of our basketball games, though I suspected Bryn was behind that. They'd been spending a lot of time together recently, and I'd noticed Kat standing close to Max all night too. I'd shot her a look when nobody was looking and she'd turned pink, making me snicker.

Jamie had been curled around Ryan on the large sofa that took up space at the back of the room and seemed happily buzzed as Max fiddled with the speakers, trying to get Jamie's song to play.

"Come on," Kit murmured, hooking his hand around my elbow and steering me toward the door.

"What is it?"

"We're getting out of here," Kit said into my ear, sending a bolt of heat through me.

"Okay," I said easily, letting him lead the way back home. I wasn't sure if he wanted to hook up, or talk, or both. Either way, this was long overdue.

We were quiet as we walked back, both a little buzzed, and Kit sniffed when I blew a cloud of strawberry vape into the air.

"When did you start smoking again?"

I shrugged. "It's been a stressful few weeks. Besides, it's only a disposable. "

He didn't say anything more about it, but I knew he disapproved. The thing was, I didn't think he cared about smoking in general, which meant he was worried about *me*. Again.

"You really do care," I said bemusedly and he shot me a look.

"Did you ever think I didn't?"

"Yes," I said honestly and he frowned.

"Well, I'm sorry. I've never not cared, Leo."

"Okay," I said and he opened his mouth, like he had something to say and wasn't sure if now was the right time.

"I need to tell you something."

Why did those words fill me with such absolute dread? "Alright," I said slowly and Kit looked at me before avoiding my eyes, sending his gaze out into the trees as we walked.

"I fucked with your parent's car."

A startled laugh flew out of me. "What?"

He pushed a hand through his hair before reaching for my hands and tugging us to a stop. "Well, more specifically, I texted Ryan and got him to fuck with your parent's car."

"Why?" I scrunched my nose, trying to make sense of what he was telling me.

"To buy me some more time. I wasn't ready to lose you."

He— "You liked pretending."

Kit huffed out a laugh and the sound was pained. "Liked it? No. It was driving me crazy. But it meant I got to hold you and touch you... kiss you." His eyes were hooded and warmth was a slow slide through my body as he stepped closer. "I wasn't sure if you actually wanted me, and I was too scared to find out."

"Scared of what?"

"You," he admitted. "Pushing you too far, too fast... I know you, Leo. You like your routines and you hate change, I just didn't want me trying to change things between us to mess with your head."

Always thinking about me. I released a slow breath and leaned in, needing his mouth on mine. "Sometimes, change is for the better."

We kissed again, a soft brush of lips that held a spark of hunger.

"Let's get back home," Kit said eventually and I smiled. I'd nearly forgotten we were standing outside—PDA clearly wasn't going to be an issue for me after all.

I nodded and we didn't speak again until we got home and made our way upstairs into his room, kicking off our shoes.

I sat on the bed beside him and waited for him to talk. We'd had the last of the walk back to think about things, I could only hope he wasn't regretting anything. He watched me in turn and licked his lips, opening his mouth and closing it like he wasn't sure where to begin, like his flow had been disrupted by what we'd spoken about outside.

"Kit," I began and he shook his head decisively.

"Right now, I don't want to talk. I just want to kiss you. Okay?"

I hesitated but then nodded. Whatever happened next, I wanted him. Whatever he was offering. It would have to be enough.

Unlike the other times we'd kissed, this was slow. Unhurried. Just for us. I tasted him, his need, his desire, on my tongue and met him breath for breath as his hands fell to my shoulders to tug me closer.

My name was a whispered prayer on his lips and I wanted to bathe in the sound, bottling it so I could hear it whenever I wanted. He peeled his tee off and over his head and helped me with mine as our hands explored lower, tracing over the ridges of our chests, learning the skin and reactions of every inch we could touch.

I reached for his zipper and his eyes closed as I palmed him, stroking his cock over his jeans before I freed him. I let my hand explore his full length slowly, tracing the veins that run down his side with my fingers before following the path with my tongue and enjoying the sound of him panting for me.

Kit tugged me upright and kissed me, harsher, rougher than before, and I met him bite for bite, moan for moan as we kicked off our trousers to leave each other bare.

I ran my hands down his body, appreciating him in the low-light of his bedside lamp, the way his hair hung low over his eye, brushing his jaw when he tilted his head back on a moan.

"I need you," he murmured and the admission broke me as we laid back against the covers and our hands found each other, stroking slowly and then faster until he grew slick beneath my hand and my hips jerked helplessly into his palm.

"Kit," I gasped and he nodded.

"Yes, yes."

I came a few moments before he did and then grimaced at the mess coating each of us. "Shower?" I offered and he nodded with a quick grin.

"Only if you'll let me wash your back."

"Deal."

I knew we needed to talk. Soon. But for now, I was going to relax and enjoy the vision that was a soapy Kit under the spray of water.

"I'm glad I can finally look at you like this," I said with a smirk. "After-game showers were... difficult."

Kit laughed as he finished rinsing his hair. "You thought you were being so sly. I know you looked, Leo. It's okay to admit it. I looked too."

"You *did*?"

"I'm only human," he murmured as I stood with him under the water. "There's only so much temptation I can take."

I kissed him, twining our tongues and biting his lip until we were both sporting semis again. I looked down ruefully and sighed.

"Sorry."

Kit grinned. "I'm not."

"You're going to run out of bedding at this rate," I said, thinking about the mess we'd made.

"I guess you'll just have to use your mouth," he said innocently, like he didn't just set my whole body aflame.

"Promises, promises," I muttered as he bent his head to kiss me again.

I was sore the next day from the amount of time Kit and I had spent devouring each other. Eventually we'd moved into my room and as the sunlight filtered in I didn't think I'd ever been so relaxed before.

Kit was asleep on my chest and I was idly stroking my fingers through his hair. It was almost as long as mine now but I still couldn't see any hint of roots peeking through.

Kit stirred and I smiled even as tension threaded through me. We hadn't spoken much last night, but now it was time. I couldn't put it off forever. "Morning."

"Hey," he mumbled. "What time is it?"

"A little after eleven."

He sighed, shifting off of me to stretch his arms above his head and I couldn't say I minded the view of his lean muscles.

"We need to talk," I said and he stilled, rolling over to face me.

"Now?"

"Yes."

He blew out a long breath but nodded. "Okay. What do you want me to say?"

I frowned. This was not how I'd expected this to start. "Well, I just want to know what we're doing here. I told you I loved you."

"Yes."

"You didn't say it back."

"No."

I blinked at him, opening and closing my mouth as I thought through what to say, my mind spinning. "Okay. I guess I understand then." I rolled away, swinging my legs to get out of bed when his next words stopped me.

"Leo, I love you."

It felt like all the air had been knocked out of me as I flopped back down onto the bed. "You do?" Bastard, messing with me like that.

"More than should be physically possible."

"So are we like, dating?"

His smile was slow but his kiss was all heat as he leaned into me. "You're mine."

I nodded but the heat in his eyes didn't dull.

"Say it."

"I'm yours, Kit."

I could feel the length of him, hardening against my hip and I moved restlessly until he kissed me into stillness again.

"I'm yours," he told me and then kissed me. "This mouth is mine." He trailed kisses down my chest and arms, sucking one of my fingers into his mouth briefly. "These are mine too." I nodded, my brain still stuck on the feeling of his tongue curling around my skin. "This cock," he said, voice rough as he reached for me and found me hard, waiting for him, "is mine."

I nodded frantically as he moved his hand over me in slow, full strokes that quickened as I bucked my hips, needing more.

"Do you want me inside you?" he murmured as I writhed. "Or do you want my mouth?"

I shook my head. "My mouth."

He raised an eyebrow before a wicked smile took over his face. "As you demand." He pulled the covers back and took my arms in his, pulling them up and over my head as he spread his legs over my chest. I moved my head forward and he chuckled. "So desperate for me." He knelt so his cock nudged my mouth and I instantly opened for him, tasting him on my tongue as he thrust deeply. "Are you going to take all of me, Leo?"

I moaned around the length of him, swallowing around his head as he rocked his hips.

"Do you want me to fuck your mouth now? Are you ready?"

I nodded my head slightly, begging him with my eyes until he rocked against me. His cock hit the back of my throat and I worked not to gag, my eyes watering even as my hips rocked, desperate for friction as the scent, the taste, of Kit filled me.

"You're going to swallow for me, aren't you," he groaned and I moaned in response, letting my tongue curl around him until his hips pumped faster, unsteadily. "Leo," he said, half-warning, half-plea, and I rocked my head forwards, encouraging him to go deep as he came in my mouth, head flung back and body trembling.

Surprisingly, I found my own release too and Kit's eyes

opened, a delighted grin forming on his mouth when he felt the hot splashes against his back as I came.

"You like to be dominated," Kit said as he pulled out of my mouth and I handed him a towel from my bedside to wipe his back.

"Sometimes," I said hoarsely and his eyes were soft when he turned back to me.

"I love you."

"I love you." I sighed contentedly, sleepiness sinking into my body again. "I guess this means I don't ever have to confess to my parents that we were fake dating all along."

Kit laughed and I joined in, seeing the ridiculousness of that statement. "We should probably tell our friends at some point though."

"Sure," I said easily, "but maybe we can keep this just for us for a while. Not hiding, no shame, I just want you all to myself for now."

"I'm good with that," he said, pushing his hair back and off of his face. "I'm pretty sure Bryn and Liv are hooking up, even if they're denying it right now. So that means almost all of our group is coupled up now, right? Crazy."

I hummed an acknowledgement as I resumed stroking his hair the way I had been before he'd woken up.

"Do you think Kat and Xander will get together? Then that would be everyone."

I hesitated. Should I tell him what I knew about Kat? It wasn't my secret to tell, but this was Kit. He wouldn't tell anyone, and everyone would know soon enough anyway if Kat was right about Max's timeline.

"I think," I said slowly, "that Xander might be with my sister."

"You think they'll do long distance?"

I shrugged. "I honestly don't know."

"And Kat? You've been hanging out with her more, right?"

"Yeah..." Kit looked at me with raised eyebrows and I grimaced. "If I tell you something, you can't tell anyone else. Okay?"

"Of course," he said, and I could tell he was intrigued.

"Kat's engaged."

Kit sat up, his mouth dropping open. "What? To who?"

"Max."

"Jamie's Max?"

I nodded and Kit whistled.

"Holy shit. I didn't even know they were a thing."

"They're not, technically. It's more of a mutually beneficial arrangement."

Kit slowly sank back down onto bed. "Well, she knows how to keep life interesting."

I laughed, but couldn't disagree.

"This is kind of perfect, right?" I said, smiling slightly as I stared up at the ceiling, enjoying the warmth of him at my side.

"Yeah," Kit mumbled sleepily and I chuckled, content to stay right where I was for the rest of the day.

My phone started ringing and I groaned, letting it go to voicemail, until three texts pinged through and I finally reached for it. So much for peace and quiet.

"Who is it?" Kit groaned and I stayed quiet as I read the messages.

"It's Kat. She signed the contract," I muttered, scrolling down to read the wall of text she'd sent over and my eyes growing wide as I got to the end. "I have to go."

"What? Why?"

"Because Kat told her parents and it was messy."

"Shit," Kit said with a sigh and I had to agree. "Go."

"Thank you." I stood up and grabbed some clothes,

throwing them on in a hurry and kissing Kit goodbye as I typed on my phone.

"I love you," he called to me and I smiled as I closed the door, off to rescue my friend from whatever mischief she'd got herself into now.

"I love you too."

Read the final instalment in the
Sun City series in 2024 with...

STILL
YOURS

ABOUT THE AUTHOR

Jade Church is an avid reader and writer of spicy romance. She loves sweet and swoony love interests who aren't scared to smack your ass and bold female leads. Jade currently lives in the U.K. and spends the majority of her time reading and writing books, as well as binge re-watching *The Vampire Diaries*.

ACKNOWLEDGMENTS

Thank you for reading Leo and Kit's story, I hope you guys loved spending time with these characters! If you want more Leo and Kit, then check out the other books in the Sun City series and **sign up to my newsletter for a fun free Bonus Scene from Strip Bare coming soon!** I'm beyond excited to get to **Kat & Max's story in 2024.** To keep up to date with my releases, don't forget to follow me on social media, Amazon, and sign up to my newsletter. **Carry on to read the first three chapters of *Get Even* for FREE!**

I'm sending so much love to my fabulous ARC team, as well as the wider bookish community for your support. Big thanks to Hannah Kaye and Jenna Weatherwax for helping me shape this book into what it now is.

Thank you to Erica from Metamorphosis Lit, without whom this book wouldn't be making its way to audio—as well as Tantor for producing it. Thanks also to Jess Amy Art for creating some gorgeous character art for my books, you nail it every time. And of course, to the lovely Brittany Keller who created such gorgeous illustrated covers for this series —thank you!

Lastly, thank you to Connor for your unending support and to my little kitty, Socks, for keeping me company while I write.

Revenge is a dish best
served hot...

GET

EVEN

CHAPTER ONE

There were a few things you should probably know. The first was that boys at college were horny. The second was that the girls were horny too. Lastly, I was a firm believer of *Don't get mad, get even*—but I also didn't like to do things in halves. That's how I ended up sandwiched between my ex-boyfriend's brother and best friend.

Brad was moaning in my ear, his breath uncomfortably hot as he pounded away underneath me, wringing small sparks of pleasure from my body. Cody echoed him like this was some kind of pack mating exercise as he moved over me, grunting as he pushed into me shallowly and then harder. The sex wasn't bad. In fact, it was highly satisfying because I knew that Aaron was going to just *die* when he found out about this. Well, maybe next time he promised he loved someone he wouldn't go ahead and fuck their best friend. *Asshole.*

Despite the moral satisfaction, my body was not hugely interested in these guys—mostly because they were idiots and I did generally like to find some sort of intellectual connection in the people I slept with. But... they were pretty, so I focused on the way Cody's golden body flexed in the mirror opposite the bed and the warmth of Brad's hands as they squeezed my breasts. I ran my hands down Brad's abs and gave him a smug smile, there were a lot of them—more than Aaron had for sure. He groaned, tweaking my nipple in one large hand as I sat up and pushed back into Cody's warmth and hardness. His breath stuttered at the change in position and I let out a moan to encourage him on and he began quickly moving again, faster this time. I took the hand Brad still had on my boob and tugged him up so I was sitting in his lap with Cody kneeling behind me, then I directed his hand downwards and pressed his fingers to my clit, giving a loud cry of appreciation. Suddenly they're both scrambling, trying to fuck me harder or faster and I rocked between them with a gasp—*finally*. Whoever said you couldn't have your cake and eat it too was wrong and revenge tasted sweet.

Cody pressed hot little kisses to my neck and heat flooded through me as I reached back and tugged at his blonde curls. I was getting close to the edge as I felt them hit a spot Aaron had never managed to find and suddenly I was shaking through my release, tightening around them until they panted in unison. Brad gripped my waist as they worked themselves to a climax too and Cody slumped against my back as he finished, hair tickling my skin until Brad eased me off them. I was a sweaty mess and I shivered as the cold air rushed over my skin, feeling oddly lonely without them pressed against me. The boys collapsed to the bed on either side of me after ditching their condoms and I smiled at them, kissing one and then the other —now for the *piece de resistance*.

"Say 'fuck me'." I giggled, brushing my dark hair away from my face and holding up my phone to take a very naked photo of the three of us looking thoroughly fucked with our sweaty, flushed skin and smug smiles. Then I found Aaron's contact and hit send, my finger hesitating for only a second over the button.

"Well, this has been fun boys—I'd say call me but, well, don't." My smile was sweet and they looked bewildered as I stood and searched the floor for my clothes—not that they covered much anyway. I'd come prepared to seduce two guys, thinking they might be a little hesitant about betraying Aaron, but really... it had taken surprisingly little effort. My phone vibrated in my hand and my stomach tightened in anticipation of his response. It had been a scant twenty-four hours since I'd got home early and found my boyfriend in my best friend's bedroom—unbeknownst to them. At first I'd gone straight to my room, sat numbly on my bed and waited for my pulse to stop pounding in my ears quite so loudly. Then I'd stood up and walked to the door, ready to burst in there, cause a scene and humiliate them both. But there was something that would hurt them more—*public spectacle.* Plus I wanted Aaron to know exactly how much he meant to his brother. *His* best friend. I'd spoken barely two words to them, just shown up in my skimpy outfit and gave Brad *fuck me* eyes and suggested he bring Cody along for the ride. That was it. They'd sold him out that quickly.

"You're leaving?" Cody asked, pushing out his full bottom lip into a pout that really was cute but dropped it when I nodded my head. I pulled on the lacy black panties I'd been wearing and Brad sat up, concern starting to muddy those big brown eyes.

"Hey, you're not going to mention this to Aaron, are you?"

I smiled. "Oh no, I don't intend on speaking to him again, but you know how he is with secrets."

Brad looked unsure about whether to be worried about his brother and Cody bit his lip. I walked a little closer and brushed a kiss across his mouth. "Wasn't it worth it though?" I asked and Cody melted, a sleepy grin pulling across his face as he decided it was, in fact, worth betraying his best friend for. I supposed I should be flattered.

A knock sounded at the door and the boys both froze like naughty kids with their hands caught in the proverbial cookie jar. I hadn't foreseen a direct confrontation with Aaron at the scene of the crime, considering he'd still been in Taylor's bedroom when I'd left over an hour ago, but this definitely could be fun.

But when I opened the door it wasn't Aaron staring back at me, it was Ryan, their other housemate. His eyes dropped to my still-bare chest and I leaned against the door frame lazily as his gaze found my see-through underwear.

"Do you always open the door in just your panties, Jamie?" he asked with a small smirk and I looked down at myself as if only just remembering my clothes—or lack thereof.

I giggled like he'd just said the funniest thing I'd ever heard. "Oh, no, I don't make a habit of it. I guess my head still isn't back in the real world yet after spending the last hour with these two." I nodded behind me to where Cody and Brad still lay naked on the bed and Ryan's mouth tightened in disapproval.

"I guess I know why Aaron's on the warpath now," he said, waving his cell phone in our direction, and the boys looked at each other in horror.

"How the fuck did he find out so fast? My dick's barely dry," Brad said and I bit back a grimace at the imagery.

"Something about a picture? I don't know, but if you don't want an awkward scene then you should probably go," he directed the last at me and I batted my long lashes at him innocently while the boys stared at me in something like shock as they realized what I'd done.

"Oh, of course. I'd hate to be an inconvenience to poor, baby Aaron."

"Essentially." Liv let out a long breath before looking up at us as though she hadn't just divulged something that was clearly pretty raw and that made something inside of me ache. I wasn't good with people or emotions, I was even worse at combining the two without the aid of alcohol or maybe some good weed. The fact that she trusted us enough to open up like that... karaoke and tequila truly were the key to starting any good friendship. "So yeah, this is all kind of new to me. Drugs, frats, karaoke and booze—like I'm not completely inexperienced but it just wasn't this... wild for me before."

Kat grinned but her eyes were as gentle as my voice had been earlier. "Well, you stick with us. This one here is particularly good at finding trouble."

I laughed as she nudged me and I squeezed Liv's hand before letting go. "I'm sorry you had to go through that, but hey, it brought you here to us—so I can't be *too* sorry." I winked and she laughed just as I'd hoped. "So where are you staying?"

"Right now I'm in temporary on-campus housing. I was supposed to be meeting someone here today about renting a room but they didn't show."

"This is perfect!" I crowed and Kat shot me a look to say I was being insensitive. I waved her off. "Well, not that they didn't show. I mean that I just kicked out my best friend for sleeping with my boyfriend, remember?"

"How could we forget? The post-revenge-hookup pic was hot." Kat laughed and I rolled my eyes.

"So, I'm saying I have a spare room I'm renting out."

"Oh my gosh, really? That would be amazing!" Liv beamed at me, her straight white teeth making me a little dizzy.

"Erm, yeah," I said, slightly dazed as the full force of that smile hit me. "We can work out the details tomorrow but you can crash at mine tonight, same for you Kat if you like."

"No, that's okay, but thanks. I should actually get home. I

Ryan looked like he almost wanted to smile until his gaze dropped to my chest again and he cleared his throat. "You might want to get dressed quickly then."

"Right, yes, it won't take me long. I wasn't wearing much when I got here."

A look of pain crossed his face that only increased as I bent over and stepped into the short black dress crumpled on the floor by the bed and found my shoes. I blew the boys a kiss and they dazedly smiled before frowning, like they weren't quite sure what had just happened and whether they were allowed to have enjoyed it.

"See you later, Ry," I said and he stepped out of the way. He was a complicated one—actually seemed to have a brain rattling around inside his pretty head and a genuine sense of humor. Fuck knows why he chose Aaron, Brad and Cody for housemates. I felt Ryan's gaze on me all the way down the hallway until I walked down the stairs and out of sight.

Sometimes, revenge was a dish best served hot. Sure, I could have walked into Taylor's bedroom, found her and Aaron tangled together and had that image burned into my brain— but I'd chosen a messier path because I wanted them to *hurt*. Aaron would hate my public fuck-you and Taylor was about to get what was coming to her too. She'd clung to me since Freshman year and I could admit that I had clung right back, I'd never had real friends before and I'd thought I'd found that with Taylor and Aaron. But the truth was, Taylor needed me more than I needed her. I'd always been independent, never really had much choice in the matter, but she had always had someone willing to bail her out, to wipe her tears or throw money at her problems. Usually her mom.

At the end of the day, Taylor was a rich white girl and her mom had taught her the most important rule: *never cause a scene.* If she knew half the shit her precious baby girl got up to...

I smirked but shook my head as I closed the front door behind me. I didn't want to involve her mom. I wanted Taylor to know what it felt like to be alone, to have the person she trusted kick her in the teeth. Figuratively, of course. I wasn't going to beat her ass, even if she deserved it, because that would make *her* the victim. I was done giving her chances or excuses. Sometimes you had to cut off a limb before the poison could spread any further and that's exactly what Aaron and Taylor felt like, poison in my veins, burning me from the inside out until all I felt was white-hot rage. Their mistake, really. The cheating would have pissed me off, but the *lying* was something I couldn't tolerate. Ever. It hit my trigger button like nothing else, probably thanks to my own, sweet mother, and practically ensured that I wouldn't have been able to stop at payback. I didn't need revenge, I needed to *win.* I smiled as my phone vibrated three more times in my hand, Aaron no doubt losing his mind over the photo and the added insult of being ignored. I didn't give a single fuck. There would be time for tears later. For now, I had to go and confront my best friend.

Aaron and I had been together for just over a year now, up until he'd made the executive decision to sleep with my best friend and roommate, Taylor. One of the big perks of the relationship was the house he shared with Brad, Cody and Ryan, it was just a ten-minute walk from campus and was so new that the boys had managed to keep it relatively clean. Though we still tended to spend more time at my place for privacy, that was how he'd met Taylor. I snorted as I followed the winding sidewalk towards the park. It had been staring me in the face, really. The long looks, the sudden silence between them when I'd walked in the room, casual touches that now represented so much more... I was an idiot. That was the hardest part. I was furious with them, but I was also so angry at myself for not seeing it sooner.

The dry heat of the Arizona air brushed against my skin pleasantly and I sighed. This wasn't a walk of shame, more like a march of victory, but from the sneers and dry amusement on a few faces it was clear nobody else got the sentiment. Then again, it was two o'clock in the afternoon on a Thursday—but revenge doesn't wait for convenience and if I'd had to sit in my room for another second, imagining what was going on across the hall, I would have murdered him. By now, he'd definitely got the message that I knew what had happened between him and Taylor and that we were over.

I smirked and finally glanced down at my phone as I walked. Three missed calls and a barrage of texts lit up the screen and I ignored them as I opened up the message app and scrolled past Aaron's bullshit to find the photo I'd sent him of the three of us simply captioned, *Touché*. I laugh reacted to his message calling me a sadistic bitch, declined another of his calls and grinned up at the sky. It was a deep blue and I inhaled the pre-summer air longingly. It was April, I was single, and this was the year *things* were going to happen. I could feel it.

Sun City in the summer was truly something else, the trees came alive and bushes, planters and shrubbery burst with color. Though, it was going to be a little less fun now that I had nobody to spend it with. I tended to run a little more on the loner side of things and now that I'd firmly kicked my boyfriend from my life (and soon my ex-bestie for good measure) my social calendar was looking a bit tragic.

My good mood faded slightly as I thought about what might be waiting for me back at my apartment. With any luck, Taylor would be out and I could deal with her later—or maybe Aaron had already warned her that I knew. I clamped down on a slightly hysterical giggle, as if Aaron gave a crap about anyone other than himself. I took a deep breath as I walked on, deciding not to think about Aaron again, I had a history paper to work on later and nothing cleared the mind and realigned the chi like a revenge threesome.

My apartment was on the other side of town, closer to the bars than it was to campus, but I didn't mind. I'd bought it for cheap when I'd moved down here in my freshman year. I'd waited before I'd come to college, working full-time at a club for a year back in Phoenix and saving every single tip I could and then scrounging it all together alongside a small inheritance that I'd been left with when my Grandmother had died. It had been enough to get me my own place and rent out the second bedroom. Aaron had helped me fix it up when we'd met, repainting the walls, sanding down floors... I sighed. I was going to have to redecorate and find a new roommate.

Taylor and I had met in our freshman year, she had been staying in the on-campus housing and I'd been friends with one of her friends. I squinted into the sun, wishing I had my sunglasses as I tried to remember the girl's name—Sara? Ivy? I shook my head and breathed a sigh of relief as I found my way beneath the canopy of trees that sheltered the long walk-way up to the main crossing that led back into town. Taylor and I had bonded over our love of karaoke on a night out and when it came time for her to re-apply for housing or find somewhere else, I'd offered to rent out the second room in my apartment to her. The rest, as they say, was history. Until she'd fucked my boyfriend.

I clamped down hard on my emotions, not wanting to shed a single tear over those two fuckwits. Tonight I was going to get rip-roaringly drunk and then tomorrow I was going to have to advertise for a new roommate.

Cocoa & Rum appeared in my eyesight and suddenly I was gasping for a bucket-sized iced coffee, never mind the fact that I was now only ten minutes away from home and could make one myself. Homemade iced coffee was never as good as the real thing and iced coffee, especially from *Cocoa & Rum*, was one addiction I did not mind feeding.

It was probably my favorite coffee house in town and as the familiar scent of coffee beans washed over me, I felt my shoulders relax. I'd actually had several messy nights here too, in the evening the place opened up into a cocktail bar with a small dance floor and the signature cocktails were to die for— and potent as hell.

The barista from behind the counter seemed new, her green-brown eyes were pretty and her smile was wide and for a second I let a hint of interest grip me. I *was* single now. If I wanted to ask out a cute girl, there was nothing stopping me... except, I couldn't risk fraternizing with the place that made the best coffee in town. That was a recipe for disaster. I placed my order and lingered at the opposite end of the counter, admiring the way the sunlight poured in through the large glass-front windows. It was only spring and already the heat was ramping up, everything starting to smell like warmth and sunlight again, maybe I'd even be able to build up my tan this summer. My olive skin was temperamental, I either became a glowy golden brown or I burnt. There was no in-between.

I accepted my coffee gratefully when the barista called my name and immediately started gulping it down as I walked slowly towards my apartment. I winced as brain freeze started to settle in and looked longingly out towards the lush green park sprawling on the walk-way behind the town. *No.* I clenched my jaw, realizing that I was putting off the inevitable. I'd had my caffeinated fortification and now it was time to face the music.

My apartment had always felt like a sanctuary and when I'd invited in Taylor, my former best friend, it had felt like a home. My Mom and I weren't close and my dad had never been in the picture, it was only really my grandmother that I'd had any real familial connection with. Then she'd died, I'd moved to Phoenix and eventually I'd ended up at Radclyffe-U.

I'd been on my way home from a class trip when I'd discovered Aaron and Taylor were boning. It was tragic how predictable it was really—came home sooner than expected and went straight to my room, intending to freshen up and surprise Aaron. Taylor had sounded... busy, in her room and I'd smirked, wondering who she'd managed to pin down now. Obviously my amusement had quickly faded away when I'd re-opened my bedroom door in time to see Aaron closing Taylor's behind him as he walked into her bedroom.

Standing outside my apartment door now, I felt the twinges of deja-vu hitting me. For this more than anything else, I hated Taylor. This was my home. *Mine.* All that security, that peace that had come with finally having something to call my own, something good I could point to and say *I did that,* had been tainted by her and Aaron's rampant fucking hormones.

I huffed out an angry breath and twisted the door handle viciously as I walked in. I was *not* going to feel like this, damn it. They were the ones who had fucked me over. Aaron was... well, I knew he wasn't going to be the forever kind of boyfriend. But Taylor? She was supposed to be my friend and that made it ten times worse.

My hallway was painted a cheerful cherry red but even the sight of the familiar walls couldn't ease the anxiety building in my chest as I stomped through and to the kitchen. I passed through the living room without a glance and it wasn't until Taylor called out that I even realized she was still here. I let out a long breath.

What the fuck? Surely she had to have heard from someone that I knew what had happened? So why was she still here? Did she think we were just going to talk it out, hug and move on? I was more likely to poop rainbows and fly around the kitchen than I was to hug it out with this fake-ass bitch.

I pasted on a smile as I scooped the drink I'd just made off of the side and strolled casually into the living room and took in Taylor, sprawled on our couch. *No.* That was *my* couch and this was *my* home. Though, Aaron had been *my* boyfriend, so clearly Taylor didn't care a lick about boundaries.

"Hey," she called again, flicking a glance away from the TV

and smiling. "Where have you been? I thought we were getting breakfast once you got back this morning."

"Yeah, sorry I had to take care of something."

"Oh?" Taylor's blonde eyebrows rose so high they almost blended in with her equally blonde hairline. "Anything interesting?"

I waved a hand airily and sipped my juice. "Just stuff between me and Aaron." That finally caught her attention and her eyes held mine, taking in my lacy black outfit with something close to jealousy passing across her face. "It's funny really..."

"What?" Did she know how curt her voice had become? Had their relationship really been staring me in the face for this long without me even realizing it?

"Well, Aaron's okay in bed—as I'm sure you know," Taylor's face whitened, her blue eyes looking bright against her deeper pallor, "but I really just didn't expect his brother to be *that* much better. Though, I suppose with Cody helping out too it evened the playing field a little."

"Jamie, I—"

"If you're about to lie to me, don't. Don't disrespect me or yourself more than you already have." My voice was cold and I felt like ice, like I was gazing at this scene from a distance and I wondered whether I would remember the minute details about this moment in the future—the tampon ad playing on the TV, the trees swaying beyond the blinds shading the window, Taylor's face, slowly clouding from horror to anger.

"I'm the disrespectful one?" Taylor stood, her blonde hair fluttering about after her like she was the heroine in a movie.

"Sorry, are you saying you *didn't* fuck my boyfriend? In my apartment?"

Taylor laughed, a sneer taking over her face as she looked me up and down. "It's not my fault that he was bored of you—I mean, who could blame him with the way you dress? Have you ever heard of that saying *giving the milk away for free?*"

Was she calling me a slut?

I didn't bother to respond to that. I liked sex. I'd previously mostly-enjoyed sex with my boyfriend. Monogamously. My current outfit was a game in seduction and not what I'd normally wear out for a walk through campus and town, so I had no idea what she was talking about and honestly? I didn't care anymore. I wanted her gone.

"Pack up your shit and get out."

Her blue eyes widened, mouth angling to catch flies as she stared. "What?"

"You thought you could bang my boyfriend, call me a slut instead of apologizing—not that it would have helped—and still live here?" Taylor's mouth opened and closed like a fish and her eyes filled with tears, the standard way she got out of anything she found distasteful, and I folded my arms across my chest, waiting to see if she had anything else to spit out.

"Okay," I said when her silence stretched on. "Nice knowing you—well, not really, actually."

"You're kicking me out?" The whine in her voice grated along my nerves and I felt my control snapping even as I wanted to crow in triumph. This was the thing that would hit Taylor where it hurt—her privilege. Girl had never been told *no.*

"What did you think was going to happen?" Taylor looked away and I let out a short laugh. "Right, you thought I'd never find out. Just so you know, you two are both way too fucking stupid to pull that off long-term. Go and pack up your shit before I do something I might regret."

She ran past me on her way out of the living room, heading to the room that was opposite mine, and I heard her crying down the phone to someone—Aaron maybe? If she thought he was going to put her up she had another thing coming. Aaron was a dick and Taylor had been single for a *long* time, maybe I'd been stupid leaving and expecting them not to hook up.

No. I wasn't responsible for their shitty actions. I finally uncrossed my arms and took a few deep breaths, trying to fight the rising tide of anger that was warring with the newfound loneliness. I'd just lost the closest thing to family I'd had since my grandmother died. *You'll make new friends.* Sure, but it wouldn't be easy. People tended to find me a little... direct. Which was fine! But it wasn't an approach that everyone liked. I couldn't change who I was and I guess it turned out that Taylor didn't really like me very much anyway if she thought I was a slut and had gone after my boyfriend.

I sank down onto my couch, running my hand over the soft gray material and sighing. The thrill from earlier had faded and now I was left in a messy situation with even messier feelings.

"Jamie?"

I looked up, startled, to find Taylor standing in the doorway, her hair scraped up into a messy bun and her mouth scrunched up in the way that only happened when she was upset.

"What?"

"I'm sorry."

I glanced away, staring at the sun beyond the window. It was less painful than looking at the girl who was supposed to be my friend, who I'd known for two years and counting and who had screwed everything up for a quick fuck with a guy who didn't even love her. *Unless he did?* I didn't reply, just nodded slightly.

"Aaron doesn't want to see me, he won't let me stay with him and I was wondering—"

Second choice yet again, huh? "Oh, so you only apologized once you were sure my ex-boyfriend wouldn't take you in? Nice. Go and crash with those sorority girls you ass-lick twenty-four-seven—I don't care, but I want you gone. Sooner rather than later if I'm going to have any chance of getting the stink of desperation out of the furniture."

I finally looked up and found the space where she'd stood empty. Good. Who needed liars and cheaters in their life anyway? I grabbed the remote from the coffee table and flicked the TV off, it was playing a Vampire Diaries re-run and right now I didn't want to have to look at Damon Salvatore's perfect face—it would only make me feel worse about my own messed up romantic life. Though, of course, if Damon Salvatore walked into a bar and asked for a vein I'd *gladly* let him tap that.

A different set of familiar blue eyes floated through my head unexpectedly and I shook my thoughts free of Ryan's killer lashes and toe-curling smirk. It wasn't the first time I'd had to do so, but he was off-limits. Fellow co-captain of the football team and Aaron's 'nemesis' (Aaron's words, boys were fucking dumb, like *seriously*, nemesis?)—unfortunately, Ry was also an absolute smoke show. I'd avoided him as much as possible when I had been dating Aaron, which had been hard considering they lived together. I didn't really understand why, considering they seemed to hate each other's guts. Men. Can't live with them... well. I guessed I'd manage.

I sank back against the couch, listening to Taylor crying down the phone to someone else in the other room as she rustled bags and clattered about. My hands shook and my eyes fluttered closed. How had my life become this cluster fuck of such epic proportions? I bit my lip as the emotion I'd been holding back finally threatened to overwhelm me and a tear trickled down my cheek, followed by another. I'd give myself a few minutes to cry and that was it. They didn't deserve my tears and these were for myself anyway, for whatever came next. For the uncertainty that the future now held without Aaron and Taylor in it. Taylor's door creaked open and I dashed the tears from my face quickly, setting my jaw and not even flinching when the front door opened and then closed. I stood and walked through the hall to Taylor's room. Clothes were strewn across the floor, make-up littered her desk as if she'd upended her bag and a suitcase sat on the bed waiting to be filled. All that was left of a two-year friendship.

The front door opened and I turned away as Taylor walked in.

"Jamie, please—" Taylor tried again and I walked into my bedroom, closing the door firmly behind me and resting my back against it as the sounds of Taylor packing resumed.

They say the best way to get over someone was to get under someone else—I could tick that off the proverbial list. Now, it was onto phase two of *Erase Aaron Matthews From My Brain/Heart:* getting ferociously drunk. I could only hope he would take the memory of my best friend with him.

CHAPTER THREE

The Box was loud on a Friday night, that was why Thursdays were my favorite day to come. There were several reasons why *The Box* was one of my favorite places in Sun City: firstly, the booze was cheap. Secondly, it looked pretty, with a flower wall along one side and pink lighting that deepened to red as the evening wore on. Lastly, their karaoke and live music nights. I loved to sing, so Wednesday nights I was usually here, setting up my guitar and ready to belt out whatever cover I'd been working on that week. I was a regular and Kat, the bartender working tonight, eyed me worriedly as I threw back my third tequila shot since I'd walked in ten minutes ago. We didn't know each other that well beyond the odd drunken ramble at the bar and the one night that we'd done karaoke together, but I liked her. Kat was honest if nothing else and she had let me rant to her about Aaron when I'd invited him to watch me sing at open mic night and he'd blown me off. I gave her a tight smile and patted her hand. "It's been a long day, babe. Keep 'em coming."

She squeezed my hand and refilled the shot glasses, waving

away my card as I reached out to pay. "This one's on me, okay? Let me know if you need anything, Jay."

My smile wobbled and I quickly grabbed another shot, downing it and then smiling widely. "You're the sweetest, thank you Kat." *See? You have more friends than Taylor and Aaron.* I groaned. I'd gone almost an hour without thinking about either of them while I enjoyed the sunset and walked to *The Box*. How drunk did I need to be before I wouldn't be able to remember their names?

Kat gave me one of her trademark sweet smiles, green eyes crinkling at the corners and cheeks dimpling, before she moved off to serve someone else.

I liked to people watch, sometimes it was nice to be surrounded by people and yet be completely alone in your thoughts—it sounded emo as fuck, but there was something peaceful about it. Usually, anyway. Tonight my thoughts were a swirling mess of *What did I do wrong? Am I really so unbearable?* And oddly and most stupidly of all, *Ryan saw me naked.*

I ran a hand through my short hair in agitation, a mixture of irritation and confusion dogging me. Who gave a singular fuck what Ryan Sommers thought?

"Come on, baby, I'd love to have your number. You look lonely."

The smarmy voice cut through my inner monologue and I rolled my eyes, glancing to my right to find the owner of that voice sitting two stools down. He was a skinny, greasy looking guy with a long face and dark hair with too much gel. He'd been attempting to sweet talk the pretty girl sitting next to me for the last ten minutes and her replies had become more and more clipped each time the guy ignored her clear signals to back the hell off. Maybe it was the tequila, maybe it was the frustration that continued to make my blood hum at the thought of Ryan, but I turned and leaned forward, draping my arm around the shoulders of the girl next to me.

She tensed momentarily before looking at me out of the corner of her eye and relaxing, apparently deciding I wasn't here with the creep harassing her. The guy frowned at me like he'd only just noticed I was there on the other side of her and *holy hell* I could see why. She'd been facing the other way the entire time I'd been sitting here, watching the door, so this was my first good look at her and I felt a brief stab of pity. She must get assholes fawning over her all the time. With her honey-hued skin, deep brown eyes and glossy hair ,she would be considered gorgeous—throw in the full lips, long legs that were currently crossed demurely in her tight jeans and curves for days and she was a knock-out.

"Have you finished playing yet, doll?" I cooed in her ear, loudly enough for the sleaze to hear me.

"Excuse me?" he spluttered, eyes bulging like a frog and a bit of spittle hit the bar.

"You're excused," I said, smiling brightly, pouting my red lips for full effect as he stared at me in shocked silence.

"Who the hell do you think you are?"

"Hers," I answered, linking my other arm around the brunette's neck and staring intently into her eyes as I leaned in, pausing as I hovered over her mouth and letting her close the distance if she chose. I could feel her stuttered breaths ghosting over my lips lightly before her mouth pressed to mine in a kiss that I deepened after a few seconds, letting my tongue briefly stroke across hers before pulling back. "Satisfied?" I said breathlessly without looking away and saw the sleazeball leave out of the corner of my eye.

"Very," the girl murmured and I laughed, pulling away. "I'm Olivia, but since you just had your tongue in my mouth, you can call me Liv."

"Nice to meet you," I said, settling back onto my own stool and ordering a cocktail from the other bartender, whose name I didn't know. "My name's Benjamin, but you can call me Jamie."

"That's... unusual?"

I gave her a wry smile and thanked the bartender a moment later as he placed the Sex on the Beach down in front of me. "My Mom thought she was having a boy and decided to keep the name regardless."

Liv let out a laugh that drew a few appreciative glances her way as her long brown hair swayed with the movement. "Wow. Well, thank you for... kissing me, I guess?"

I smirked. "Happy to be of service. Are you meeting someone?" I half-hoped she'd say no—and not just because the kiss had been good. I could use the company and it would be... nice to meet some new people. Not a thought I often had, but I was putting it down to the alcohol and the shitty forty-eight hours I'd just lived.

"Oh." She glanced down at her hands folded in her lap, her lashes were long and full and I realized that though I would happily take her back to my place, I could use a friend more than a fuck buddy right now. "Yeah, but I don't think they're going to show." She had a light accent that might have been Southern and her apparent worry made the twang thicken. I smiled and gestured for Kat to bring over another cocktail.

"Well, that's their loss and my gain I guess!" I dropped her a wink as Kat set her drink down. "Tell me, do you like karaoke?"

Three more cocktails, two shots ,and a timeless rendition of Careless Whisper later, I'd told Liv and Kat (who had joined us at nine once her shift had ended) what had gone down with Aaron and Taylor.

Kat shook her head. "I never liked him. He's too..." Liv and I leaned closer to Kat as she took a long sip of her mojito, "cookie-cutter. Like, you know when you see guys in ads that are supposed to be super clean cut and all-American?"

I nodded as I bit down on the lime and almost choked laughing at the face Olivia made after taking her tequila shot. "Yeah I get that. He's the other sort of all-American though— Mr. Nice Guy. Except, he does coke in the evenings and thinks grinding to music is dancing."

Liv looked horrified as Kat burst out laughing. "Is that... common?"

"What?" I raised an eyebrow. Liv seemed... innocent. I mean, not prudish or anything, just like she maybe wasn't that experienced. Her mouth had hung open for a solid five minutes after I'd told her about my revenge sex that afternoon.

"The drugs," Liv whispered. Except, we were all pretty drunk so she wasn't really that quiet. Even Kat was keeping pace, the five tequila slammers had definitely helped her catch-up to our level.

"Liv, I'm going to ask you something and I don't want you to be offended or anything because the answer doesn't really matter that much."

"Okay," she said, biting down on her lower lip.

"Are you a freshman?"

Liv gasped and Kat howled, though that might have been because a squeeze of lime juice shot in her eye. "I am *not* a Freshman."

I raised my hands in supplication and fluffed my fringe off my face with my hand. God was it just me or was it boiling hot in here? "I said not to get offended! It's just that this all seems very new to you."

"That's because it is." She shrugged lightly. "I'm in my second year. I just transferred to Radclyffe from St Agatha's."

Kat and I blinked at her in shocked silence before I managed to make my tongue work again. "You transferred out of one of the most strict religious schools in the US to a college named after a lesbian?"

"Well, sort of. I was actually kicked out." Oh my god. Who *was* this new friend I'd made?

"Spill," Kat said, eyes glittering dangerously as she sensed good gossip and I shot her a warning look.

"Why were you kicked out?" I made my voice gentle. It wasn't a tone I used often.

"Um, I got caught having sex."

I was pretty sure I gasped aloud. "You have to be chaste at St Agatha's?"

"Not really, I mean they prefer no sex before marriage. Like, *heavily* prefer it. But it was who I was caught sleeping with that was the issue."

"You're killing me here," Kat whined and I frantically shushed her.

"Was it a teacher?"

"I mean, that certainly didn't help." I wasn't sure my eyes could get any wider. Had I really said I thought she wasn't very experienced? "But it was more the fact that she was a girl that was the nail in my coffin. My parents screamed down our halls of residence and the Matron decided it would be best if I transferred out to another school of my choice with a full scholarship, since my parents were now refusing to pay my tuition."

Holy shit. She'd caused a lesbian scandal at one of the most religiously zealous colleges around, Olivia might just be my new hero. I grabbed for her hand and clasped it in mine. "They tried to give you hush money?"

have an early lecture tomorrow, but we should do this again sometime." Kat smiled and it eased something in my chest that had been hurting since I'd heard Taylor's door close and watched Aaron disappearing inside, clad in just boxers.

"I'd love that," I said and smiled when she grabbed my phone and input her number before doing the same for Liv and waving goodbye. "Guess we should be buying that dickwad from earlier a drink, right? Who knew sticking my tongue in your mouth would be so fortuitous—but I'm leaving here slightly less angry and with two new friends." I wasn't usually a huge sharer and in that moment I remembered why I didn't drink tequila anymore, but I had a good feeling about Liv, she seemed genuine and nice and maybe a little naive. Like she needed someone just as much as I did.

Liv laughed. "I'd say we're both due for a little luck, right?"